GHOST TRAPPED

VALLEY GHOSTS SERIES BOOK 3

BL MAXWELL

COPYRIGHT

Dedicated to all the ghost hunters, and lovers of the paranormal. Happy Haunting.

Valley Ghosts Series Book Three

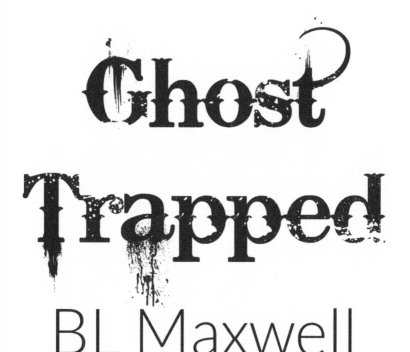

Ghost Trapped

BL Maxwell

CHAPTER ONE

WADE

"I GUESS IT'S OFFICIAL, we're in the ghost hunting business." Jason smiled over at me as we drove away from the restaurant in Old Sacramento.

"So, do we get to have matching jackets? Maybe shirts?" I teased, then turned in time to see Jimbo roll his eyes.

"We need a name first, a really good name." Jason rubbed his chin in thought.

"Oh boy," Jimbo breathed out as he turned to look out the window.

"Basement Dwellers Ghost Hunting?" Jason suggested.

"Little long, don't you think?" I commented, but he didn't stop suggesting even more names that were no better than the first few.

"Unchain the Spirit."

"Specter Squad."

"Specter Detectors."

"Mostly Ghostly."

"Spooks R Us?"

He really had lost his mind, but that didn't stop him.

"Spectrally Challenged, Haunt Helpers, Soul Chasers, Phantom . . . something."

"My god!" Jimbo commented.

"Apparition Alleviation, Kelpie Keepers . . ."

"What the hell's a kelpie?" I asked. "No matter what name we choose, we're basically running scared as soon as shit happens—wait, that's it! Running Scared Paranormal Research." I slapped the steering wheel and nodded to punctuate that decision.

Jason and Jimbo both rolled their eyes in answer. "Yay, so it's official, we're Running Scared?" I said.

"Fine. But we won't be running this time," Jason said.

"Speak for yourself, Jason," Jimbo added with a sniff.

"Dude, you do realize we had to drag you into The Vineyard House, and then one of us had to keep a hand on you at all times to make sure you didn't run screaming into the night," I reminded Jimbo as I met his narrow-eyed glare in the rearview mirror.

"Fine, whatever. Running Scared it is," Jimbo snapped back.

"Fine," I countered.

"So, do I get no say in this whatsoever?" Jason asked.

"No," we both barked at him.

"I guess it works. It describes you two perfectly," Jason said with a huge grin.

Jimbo rolled his eyes again, then muttered, "Whatever. But I'm not wearing a shirt that has Running Scared printed all over it."

"Who says it would be 'printed all over it'?" Jason asked, and settled back into his seat.

"Yeah, we just need a logo, nothing huge," Jimbo added from the back seat.

"Just a logo? You two have lost your freaking minds."

"We'll see what your mom thinks." Jason effectively ended the conversation with that statement. There was no way my mom wouldn't absolutely love the idea, and knowing her, we'd have shirts, business cards, and pens printed up within twenty-four hours.

We had just finished our first official meeting with a client about a haunting in his business. Dean was the manager of The Hitching Post, a popular new restaurant in the Old Sacramento area. The whole time the business had been open he'd suspected they had a ghost, but so far it had been more mischievous contact than harmful—moving a glass or napkin to a different spot, hiding a fork, only to have it returned the next day to the exact spot. That kind of nonthreatening stuff.

It was only after one of the waitresses was trapped down in the lower level for hours and left terrorized by what she'd experienced that he decided he needed our help. He explained he'd seen a story about our adventures on the news and was desperate enough to find out exactly what he was dealing with, so decided to give us a call.

"Hey, Jimbo, what's up with you and Dean, the manager?" I asked, looking back at him.

He stared straight ahead, not bothering to act like he'd even heard me talking to him.

"Jimbo? What the fuck?" Jason turned and looked at him. "Is there something you need to tell us, about how you know Dean Peterson?"

"I don't need to tell anybody anything. It's my own damn business."

Jason stared hard at him for a full minute, before Jimbo squirmed a little then started to speak. "Fine, we may have been in culinary school at the same time."

"No way, what was that, like, fifty years ago?" I asked, knowing full well it would get a reaction.

"Fuck you, Wade. It wasn't that long ago," he snapped back in his usual snarky way. "And that's all you need to know."

"Oh, so there's some history there, huh?" I pressed, knowing it would piss him off.

He folded his arms and once again clammed up, looking out the window as we drove back home. "I wonder if Mom knows about your history with Dean?" I said as nonchalantly as I could, and held in a grin when I saw Jimbo's gaze snap away from the window to stare a hole into the back of my head. He noticed I was watching him through the rearview mirror, and he huffed out a breath while doing his best to ignore me again.

I smiled over to Jason and put my hand on his leg. "So, do you think we can help Dean? No one seemed to be in a hurry to go down into the basement there."

"I think so, we'll need to do some research and find out what all those people are doing down there. Jimbo, would your sister help us if we need it?"

We'd found out that Jimbo and his sister were both powerful in their own right—Jimbo was a beacon, someone ghosts were drawn to, where his sister was a strong psychic, and able to communicate with the spirits in a way neither Jason or I could.

"I have no clue, you'll need to ask her yourself," he huffed, actually huffed.

I stopped at a light and turned to look at him straight on and laughed. "Jimbo, you make it so hard to take you seriously when you're always in such a grouchy mood."

"What the fuck are you talking about?" He squinted. "I'm always Mr. Personality, ask anyone. Your mom would be pretty pissed if she knew you were giving me shit." He raised his chin to accent the line of crap he was trying to sell us.

"Just because my mom thinks you're 'adorable,' doesn't mean I agree. And you're way nicer to her than you are to anyone else. Even Dean, who you lied to us about knowing."

"Leave him alone, Wade," Jason said as he patted my shoulder.

"Yeah, listen to your boyfriend," Jimbo snapped at me, taking full advantage of the situation.

"You know your mom will get it out of him, and she won't be able to keep it to herself. The things that woman has shared are truly embarrassing," Jason said, and turned around to look right at Jimbo.

Jimbo tried to give him a dirty look but ended up looking horrified. "That woman has told me details about the two of you I'd rather forget," he mumbled.

"Yep, that's my mom. And just imagine what she'll tell us after you tell her about Dean—and you *know* you'll tell her. She should work for the government, that woman can make anyone talk," I said.

"You have no idea," Jimbo mumbled, again with a huff.

We pulled up to my house, and Mom was right out front, watering the plants as usual.

"Hey, Mom," I called out as I closed the car door and walked toward her.

"Hey, baby, how'd it go? I want to hear all about it." She turned off the water and rushed over to the front door. Jason and Jimbo followed us in, and we all took our usual seats in the living room.

"Well, don't keep me waiting," she said, waving her hands in anticipation.

"Oh, we thought of a name for the business. What do you think of Running Scared Paranormal Research?" Jason asked.

"Can we have shirts?" she asked immediately, sitting on the edge of her seat.

"Sure, whatever you want," he answered.

"I thought we agreed no shirts," Jimbo said.

Jason gave him a slow smile before he spoke. "You might want to ask Jimbo about who our new client is first," he said, changing the subject and throwing Jimbo under the bus with one sentence.

My mom's gaze locked on Jimbo and he squirmed a little. "Fuck you, Jason."

"James, you know I don't want to hear that language, now spill, who was the client?"

"His name is Dean Peterson, he's the manager of The Hitching Post, and him and Jimbo have some super-secret past that he won't tell us about," Jason revealed as he threw Jimbo further under the proverbial bus.

Mom's head snapped back around to face Jimbo, and she pinned him with a stare he visibly flinched away from.

"So, James, care to tell us the whole story?" she asked, voice as sweet as could be.

"Oh for the love of—fine! I met him when we were in culinary school. He was just starting out, and I was just beginning my last few courses. That's it."

"There's nothing else you want to tell us?" Mom pushed, moving to sit next to Jimbo. She took his hand in hers, and he melted a little; he really had a soft spot for her.

"Well, we might have had a moment," he said with a fond smile and a shake of his head.

"Come on, James, you know I want all the details." She smiled at him then and leaned on his arm, and to my surprise, he smiled back at her. A rare occurrence for this professional grouch.

"We might have hooked up once or twice," he said, his hand partially covering his mouth and muffling his words.

"What?" Jason jumped up. "Why didn't you tell us that? I thought maybe you two worked together, or you had a bad time with him at culinary school. And why are you grinning, Wade?"

"This is gonna be so good," I breathed out and tried to hide my excitement with a wide smile.

"I hate you all so much," Jimbo grumbled, before smiling at Mom, who smiled back at him and looped her arm with his then rested her head on his shoulder.

"Okay, James, I want all the details, now."

CHAPTER TWO

JASON

WE DROVE AWAY from our meeting with Dean. Jimbo's reaction to him was so bizarre, the man didn't seem to like anyone, well, besides Wade's mom. Yet there had to be something between him and Dean for him to react the way he did. It was amusing and weird, but not as weird as what had met us in the basement of The Hitching Post. As soon as we'd entered the dirt-floored space, I could feel all the spirits that were trapped there—all of them in pain, fearful, and wanting desperately to leave but not being able to.

They were trapped. Someone, or something, was keeping them there, and we'd need to figure out what that was before it would be safe for anyone to go into the basement of Dean's business.

I tried to join in with Wade and Jimbo as they harassed each other, but I was so distracted by what I'd felt, I had a hard time concentrating.

Wade parked in front of his house, and we all sat in his living room, watching on as his mom interrogated Jimbo. She was an expert, as Wade and I both knew, and he cracked in no time at all, but all the while my mind kept wandering back to the basement.

"Hey, are you okay?" Wade asked, pulling me in closer to his side.

I hesitated for a moment before answering. "Yeah, I'm just thinking about what I sensed when we were in the basement. Did you feel it too? There were so many, I couldn't separate them, there were just too many."

"I felt it too—fear, panic, and confusion. I don't think they understand why they're trapped there. I don't understand it either. They can't all be from one flood or event, that's not possible," Wade said.

"I'm not sure, it doesn't seem like they'd all *choose* to stay," I said.

"What are you two talking about?" Wade's mom asked.

"Sorry, I can't get it out of my mind. There were so many spirits in that basement. Jimbo, could it be they were all attracted by you?" I asked.

He thought for a second before he answered. "I've spent years blocking that part of me. I keep my walls up all the time. I know for a fact, when we were in there, I was not open to attracting spirits. I kept myself hidden from them."

"Do you think your sister would be willing to visit there? Maybe she can communicate with some of them, give us an idea what we're getting into." I hoped she'd be willing to help, this felt different to me. Of all the places we'd been to that had been haunted, none of them felt this suffocating.

"I'm not sure, she tries to stay in control, and if you're right and there are a lot of spirits, it may overwhelm her."

"That can happen?" I asked. I knew psychics were vulnerable to the powers some ghosts possessed, but I also knew his sister had said she had protections against it.

"With that many, I'm not sure. We'll need to ask her if she's interested or willing."

"It's so exciting to see you guys all working together. I feel like I'm living in a crime novel, or something crazy like that," Mrs. Rivers said as she leaned on Jimbo. He didn't even flinch anymore. He'd learned, like we all did, that it was easier to just go along with her.

"We'll need to do more research on events that have happened in that area. We know there was a flood or two, which led to mass casualties, but I'm not sure about more than that."

"Why don't you boys go take the underground tour? My friend went on it and said it was very interesting, and she's not even interested in ghosts. There is quite a history in that area, apparently," Mrs. Rivers said.

"I'm not going on a tour," Jimbo snapped.

"Oh hush, James, it'll be good for you, it's educational," she scolded.

"Great idea," I said, and opened my phone to find out when the tours were scheduled. "It looks like they have a few tours daily, is everyone going?" I looked at them all. Jimbo rolled his eyes, Wade looked a little hesitant, and his mom looked at me with wide-eyed wonder before her hand shot up.

"I want to go," she announced.

"You don't have to raise your hand. I'll go, you know I'm not letting you go without me," Wade said as he reached for my hand. I smiled and leaned into him, before looking over to Jimbo.

"Fuck, I guess I'm not getting out of this one," he grumbled. Mrs. Rivers smacked him on the arm, and he cleared his throat. "Sorry, I meant to say, I'd love to go."

"Much better, James, now when are we going?" Mrs. Rivers asked.

"How about now?" I suggested, hoping they'd agree, and wouldn't protest, as we'd just driven back from that area.

"Might as well get it over with," Wade said, making me laugh.

"Might as well," I said.

CHAPTER THREE

WADE

WE ALL LOADED into the car and headed back to Old Sacramento. The directions said to meet at the railroad museum, so after finding a parking space, we walked over and joined the small group already gathered. It was a warm day, not uncomfortable, but I thought for a moment about how things would be cooler once we were underground. I stepped closer to Jason and brushed his fingers with my own. He turned to me and smiled before taking my hand and weaving our fingers together.

A man dressed in period clothing, including a top hat and a waistcoat, walked over to the group and introduced himself as the tour guide. "This is so exciting," Mom said as we all followed him to the first stop on our tour. The tour guide explained how many times this area had flooded and then been rebuilt. How it started as a tent city, and finally was built with more permanent structures, but those had been nearly destroyed when there was a flood that changed the landscape, leaving a huge lake in its place for several months. It had rained for forty-three days straight, and left the valley flooded, from Redding to Bakersfield. It was unknown exactly how many had died, but it was in the tens of thousands, according to the guide.

We made our way into the first area that would take us underground; this was one of the buildings that had been lifted in hopes of saving the city if another flood were to happen. We stepped in, and the smell of dank earth and rot seemed to permeate the place. I was hit with the feeling of being trapped, and felt a bead of sweat roll down my back.

Jason squeezed my hand and looked at me with concern. "Are you okay?" he whispered to me.

"I'm okay, just a weird feeling is all."

"If you get uncomfortable and want to leave, let me know. We don't have to do this," Jason said.

"Are you boys okay?" Mom asked as she leaned in close to us both, and Jimbo looked between us with a serious look.

"You need to learn how to block them," he said.

"What are you talking about?" I asked.

"You know what I'm talking about. If I didn't close off myself to them, they'd all be here, and you'd really be miserable. You're feeling a small part of what's really here. I felt it at the restaurant, but not like this." Jimbo leaned in close as he said this, not wanting to alarm the other people on the tour.

To say I was alarmed would have been an understatement. My nerves were stretched tight, and every little movement or noise made me want to flinch. I squeezed Jason's hand, relieved he was so close and I could touch him without worrying what his reaction would be.

"If you want to leave, we can leave," Jason said again, looking into my eyes with that same intensity I was used to seeing from him when he was talking about his latest paranormal mystery.

"I'm okay, but I think Jimbo's right, I need to start

working on how to control what I feel when I'm in a place that has a lot of activity."

"Is it worse since The Vineyard House?" he asked.

"Yeah, I used to just feel nervous, but I thought it was just that. Me being nervous. But this is more intense. I feel like I'm crawling out of my skin," I said to Jason.

"Everything okay over here?" the tour guide asked, drawing everyone's attention to us.

"Yeah, we're fine, thanks," Jason answered.

"Okay then, let's move on to the next stop, I think everyone will like it. Where this is a small area, the next one is huge. It was where many businesses once were, after the building above had been lifted. They used that newly created area for their businesses. Sadly, when it flooded again, most of them were washed away, or drowned under the building."

We walked out of the small area and I took a deep breath of fresh air, as we followed him down one of the small cobblestone-lined alleys, until we came to the back wall of one of the larger buildings that faced the main street. He slid open a barn-type door, revealing a space that was cavernous. The ceilings were low, and the braces and piers they'd set in place after jacking the building up were still standing. The crushing weight of the building was tangible, and obvious in the timbers that were bowed under the weight they supported. But that wasn't the only weight I could feel.

"Jason, it feels so heavy in here. I know you felt it in the basement at the restaurant, but this is something else." The heaviness made me cringe away from the space, the only thought on my mind getting the fuck out of there.

"Babe, let's get you out of here. I'm not sure what's happening, but you can't stay." We'd barely crossed into the big open space. It was sectioned off to keep the public from falling into the areas where they'd been excavating, most likely looking for hidden treasures left behind from the distant past.

"No, I want to stay, I'll be okay."

"Dude, let me talk to you for a second," Jimbo said, and took my arm and led me over to the side, away from the rest of the group, who were spreading out and exploring the area. "You have to visualize, imagine putting a wall around your consciousness. Imagine there not being any weak areas for someone or something else to enter. You need to protect your mind, or they'll get in and fuck with you."

I nodded and took a deep breath. Closing my eyes, I visualized a strong barrier around myself, a bright light surrounding me and keeping me safe. I felt Jason take my hand, but I still kept my eyes closed. I could do this.

"I'm sorry, Wade, I didn't know this would be so hard on you," he whispered close to my ear. I looped my arm around him and pulled him close.

"I didn't either, I think it must be all the energy trapped under here. I probably left myself open to feel it, after what we experienced before . . . it's like that experience opened something in my mind I can't control."

"You'll be okay, we'll figure it out together." He leaned in closer to me, and somehow, I knew he was giving me strength to keep myself safe.

My eyes slowly opened, and he was right there with a worried look on his face. "I'm okay, let's see what else we can learn. But stay close, it's easier to block out the feelings when you're closer."

"You'd have to drag me away," he said, and kissed the side of my head. "Let's catch up with the tour. Oh, and

Jimbo, thanks." Jimbo nodded to us both then walked back to where Mom waited.

"Everything okay, guys?" she asked, weaving her arms through ours.

"Yeah, Mom, we're fine." Jason looked behind her and met my eyes. I gave him a smile I didn't feel and hoped we really were okay.

CHAPTER FOUR

JASON

SOMETHING WAS WRONG. Wade had never been affected by any of the places we'd visited before. He was great at reading people, very aware of their emotions. But he had never felt the presence of spirits.

"How are you feeling?" I asked as we followed the rest of the group to explore the underground area.

"I'm fine, I'm not really sure what came over me," Wade answered.

"You know exactly what came over you, Wade, that's what I'm trying to tell you. Once you open up that door you can't close it," Jimbo said, his normally brusque manner now gone. He was clearly concerned.

"Jimbo, you don't know it was anything like that, maybe he just doesn't feel well? It's hot down here, I was expecting it to be cooler, maybe he's dehydrated. Speaking of—do you need something to drink?" Fuck, now *I* was concerned.

"Jason, I'm fine, I just felt weird for a while, but now it seems to be gone." I knew him well enough to know he was lying, I just didn't understand why, or what, exactly, had happened to him. I could sense there were many spirits down here—some were here because they wanted to stay, but I wasn't sure why some seemed unable to leave. Maybe they stayed because they felt some pull to finish their existence out where they'd worked so hard for a new beginning. I had no way of knowing, but Jimbo's sister did.

"Jimbo, I think we need to talk to your sister. Maybe she can help Wade figure out what's happening. And if she'd be willing, maybe she could investigate the basement of Dean's restaurant and see if she gets any readings while she's down there."

"I can ask, but she's not fond of putting herself into any situation she can't control. She's had too many experiences that didn't end well in the past."

"What do you think, Wade?" I asked.

"That sounds like a good idea, I have no idea what I feel, or why I'm feeling it. I think we need someone who's experienced feelings and emotions like these before. I'm not even sure it wasn't just my response to being underground."

"You've never been afraid of being underground before, how many times did we go through the drainage pipes and wander around under the streets in the storm drains? We've been in confined areas many times, you've never reacted. This was something different," I said as I rubbed his arm, hoping to give him some comfort and support. Jimbo pulled his phone out and tapped out a text. "Can you get a signal down here?"

"One bar, I'll know soon enough if it went through." His phone pinged with a message he read before tucking it away. "Janis said to come by when we're done here. That she could feel the ripple of whatever you tapped into and we all need to meet. Fuck." He scrubbed his face and walked back to where Wade's mom stood listening to the tour guide.

"Are you okay with that? I know Janis is a little much," I asked Wade.

"I think it's a good idea. I'd like to understand what's happening, usually it's you that's the expert in all things paranormal. Are you slacking?" Wade teased, and shoved into my side.

"Nope, not slacking. I just have no clue what's happening. I could feel there were spirits around us, just like I felt it in the basement at Dean's restaurant. But this was different, and it was almost like they didn't want me to know what they were up to, or they were trying to hide." I didn't want to alarm him any more than he already was, but something was definitely going on, and I hoped Jimbo was right and Janis would know what it was and how to deal with it.

She'd warned us about this, said we needed to learn how to protect ourselves, and we hadn't listened. I was so anxious to take this job and finally start a business as paranormal researchers that I'd put Wade in danger, when Janis had known, and tried to warn us.

"I know what you're thinking, but I won't let you blame yourself. I was there when she said we needed protection, and neither of us made the effort to contact her and get some training. This is on us all. Jimbo included," Wade said.

I knew he was right, but it didn't make it any easier to accept that I'd put him in danger over something we'd known in advance.

He wrapped his arm around my shoulders and pulled me close, resting his forehead against my own. "We'll figure it out," he whispered.

There was a breathy sigh to my right, and I pulled away from Wade to find his mom and Jimbo right next to us. She had a look on her face that made me picture her with little hearts popping out of her eyes, while Jimbo just looked annoyed.

"You two are just adorable," Mrs. Rivers said. Jimbo rolled his eyes and walked toward the exit, following the rest of the group.

"Come on, let's finish this and head over to Janis's house," Wade said, pulling me along behind him. I followed him and hoped Janis really could help us like she said she could, because there was no way in hell I was putting Wade in danger. Not for anything.

We walked back to the museum where we'd started, and the tour guide thanked everyone. The four of us stood there for a moment while the group started to break up, wandering off to do other things or return to their cars.

"What are you guys waiting for? Let's go talk to Janis," Jimbo said.

"Oh, can I go too? I'd love to meet your sister," Wade's mom said as she took Jimbo's arm.

"You might regret that," Wade mumbled, just loud enough for her to hear. She turned and smiled, while Jimbo shot him a dirty look, before rolling his eyes—again. We all walked back to the car, and since Janis lived close to the downtown area, it didn't take us long to get to her house. I once again marveled at how normal her house looked, with its neatly maintained yard and bright white trim, and I wondered if her neighbors had any idea who lived next door to them, and what spirits she invited into their space.

I waited for Wade to walk to my side of the car and took his hand as we walked up to the door. Jimbo again stayed behind us, as hesitant as he was the first time we'd been here. "Come in," I heard Janis call from inside before any of us could announce our arrival.

"That's so creepy," Wade whispered.

"She has a camera, dumbass," Jimbo said as he pushed past us and walked into the small house.

"Back here, James," she called from the backyard. We stepped through the house and out to her covered patio where she sat on a lounge, looking the picture of relaxation. Yep, we should have talked to her before now.

"So, I guess you realized why I warned you about learning to protect yourselves?"

"Don't lecture them, you know they don't have any experience in this shit," Jimbo said, looking between the two of us.

"Language," Mrs. Rivers and Janis both said, before turning to face each other and laughing.

"Hello, I'm Wade's mom, Deidre."

"Lovely to meet you, Deidre, I'm Janis. I'm sure James has told you all about me," she said with a warm smile. Both of them dissolved into laughter I didn't even pretend to understand, before walking farther into the backyard and chatting like two old friends.

"Do they know each other?" I asked Jimbo.

"Fuck no, they're just really enjoying the fact they're annoying the hell out of me. Two of a kind," Jimbo snapped back at me.

"Oh god, what have we done putting them together?" Wade said, shock and horror plainly visible on his face. And with that I barked out a laugh, admittedly enjoying both of their misery.

CHAPTER FIVE

WADE

I WATCHED as Mom and Janis walked around the backyard and shared an occasional laugh, while glancing at the three of us, then laughing even more. "What the hell is happening?" I thought out loud.

"This is why I try to avoid my family as much as humanly possible. My sister lives to give me crap. It's not just the whole 'we're a family of psychics' thing, it's the 'James, let me annoy you until you want to scream' thing." He scrubbed his hand down his face and flopped into one of the patio chairs.

"Well, that wasn't dramatic at all," I said as I looked between Jason and Jimbo. "Why did we come here again?"

"You need my help," Janis called from across the yard. She walked closer, and when she stood right in front of me, she took both my hands in hers. "I tried to warn you—all of you, but you didn't want to listen. I know now you weren't ready. I'm not sure all of you are at this time, but, Wade, you are. And you'll need to listen and heed what I tell you."

Jason moved closer to me and stood so close I had to drop Janis's hand to lace my fingers with his. "Can you help him? Help us all?" I looked at his expression and realized I'd seen that look on his face before, when we were at The Vineyard House.

"I can try, you'll need to work on building your mental defenses or the spirits will have their way with you. Wade, you know you're an empath, but something has changed, grown stronger. The veil has been altered, and for some reason I do not understand, there are spirits there that will try to use your gift to rip a hole into this realm."

"But why would they go after Wade?" Jason asked.

"They can sense he's been touched by the spirit world before," Janis explained.

"I was touched by them too, literally. I still don't understand why they'd target Wade."

"Your experience made you stronger, your sense of them is more clearly defined, and you know how to deal with them now. You've lost any fear you had of the spirit world. Wade, you were already afraid of all the things you could not understand, and you didn't want to know more about that side of the veil. But in a way, the experience you had split you wide open. You can't control the power they have over you, and they know it. They'll do anything they can to get your attention, in the hope of taking over your body and, perhaps, never letting you take control again," she said, her voice quiet and full of dread.

"Wha—what can I do? I could feel them earlier. There are so many down there, all of them wanting something. I'm not sure what, but they were all very blatant in wanting me to know they were there. Even at The Vineyard House, it didn't feel so menacing. They all want something." I thought back to the feeling of dread I'd felt in the basement, and a cold chill ran through me at what that might mean.

"You know what they want. You may not want to admit it, but don't discount your gut feeling. You're not wrong."

"What you said before was the truth. They want me, they want to take over my body and never give me back control. Those are the thoughts that kept running through my mind while we were down there. If they had the chance to do it, I'd never get the chance to be free again." I blinked before turning back to face Jason, and the blood seemed to drain from his face.

"Wade, you're mine. I don't give a fuck what they want. You fought for me, and now I'll fight for you. If they think you'll go willingly, they have no clue what a fight they're in for," Jason said as he cupped my jaw. I covered his hand with mine and breathed him in.

"What do we need to do?" I asked Janis.

"You'll need to cleanse your spirits, both of you. Clear out anything negative that could affect you when you're dealing with spirits or anything to do with the spiritual realm."

"How do we do that?" I asked.

"I know what do to," Jason spoke up. "Do you think smudging would be enough?"

Janis put her finger to her lips in concentration before looking at Jason. "No, you'll need to gather a smudge stick, a white candle, salt, and water. Choose a space that is peaceful for the two of you. Someplace in your home that makes you happy, and where you feel love. Arrange the candle to the south, the smudge stick to the east, salt to the north, and a bowl of water to the west."

"Wait, let me write this down," I said as I took out my phone and tapped out the directions she'd described.

"Put an empty bowl in the center, sit on the floor, one of you at each end. Center yourself, clear your mind, and imagine the outcome you'd like: to be cleansed of all negative energy and to be filled with white light that can protect you. Light your candle and continue thinking those thoughts until your candle goes out. It's best if you don't extinguish it. It will go out when you have achieved spiritual cleansing. Visualize that the negativity will be trapped in the bowl in the center, the salt and water will help focus it away."

"How will we know if it's worked?" Jason asked.

"You'll know, you don't realize how much of the weight of the veil you carry with you. All will be lifted after the cleansing."

"Is that all we need to do?" I asked. It was weird, but it was easy.

"No, you'll need to get some protections, otherwise you'll be infected again as soon as you encounter any spirits. Which if you're going to continue to keep company with this one, it's only a matter of time before you're exposed again," she said, pointing her finger at Jimbo. He squinted at her and took a deep breath before he said anything.

"You know I keep it closed down. I can't help it if those assholes see me no matter how much I tone it down."

"I know, James, it's a blessing and a curse. I'm proud of you for continuing to practice your safeguards. You've become quite adept at keeping them at bay. But as I have said before, nothing you do will completely hide you from them, your beacon is a shining star in their darkness. They'll always search you out, and you must never let down your guard," she warned.

Jimbo went a little pale and met my eyes for a moment. He was worried, it was plain to see. This was one of the few times he didn't have a sarcastic response. I realized I would have done anything to hear him offer one of his patented stinging comments.

"You should both get a grounding stone, it will help keep you centered in times of stress and chaos of spirit. Give me a moment and I'll tell you which stones would be best for you." She guided us to sit on a chaise lounge, and after closing her eyes, she held her hands above our heads, and seemed to be listening for some sign that none of us could see.

"Jason, for you I think black tourmaline, you must always carry it with you in your right front pocket. It will help ground you and dispel any negativity you encounter."

"And where will I find this miraculous stone?" Jason asked. Hs annoyance surprised me. He was usually really into learning about anything that involved the spirit world.

Janis smiled at him with her always serene smile. "I have it for you right here." She opened a small cloth bag that held many stones, and flicked through them until she found the one she wanted. She handed it to Jason, and after he looked at it then showed it to me, he shoved it in the right front pocket of his shorts.

I waited to see what stone she'd pick for me. She once again closed her eyes, and for a moment her eyebrows pinched together; something was worrying her. I glanced at Jason to find him already looking at me. He squeezed my hand as Janis opened her eyes and once again sorted through her bag of stones. "Wade, for you, I choose red jasper. It will give you strength and help with your emotional endurance. I fear you will need all the strength you can get for what comes next."

"What comes next?" I asked.

She just gave us a knowing smile and turned to walk into the house.

CHAPTER SIX

JASON

WE ALL LOOKED at each other, and Wade's mom looked more worried than she had before, even when we were on the tour of the underground.

"Don't worry, Janis knows what she's doing. She'll tell us how to power up and protect ourselves, we'll all be fine," Jimbo said, mostly to Deidre. "She won't let any harm come to them, they'll be safe."

"It's not just them, I'm worried about you too," Deidre said as we walked into the house. Janis sat at her table, tarot cards laid out in front of her. She shuffled them before slowly laying them out in front of her.

"What does it say?" Jimbo asked.

"It won't be easy, first you'll need to go to the basement at the restaurant. There you will do a cleansing ceremony. It may not be as easy to cleanse this space as it will be in your own home, and it may take several times. The three of you should be in the spirit circle, along with the owner of the restaurant. You'll need the help of someone who is tied to the building. And for your own sakes, bring your stones, you will need them."

"You're sure Wade won't be hurt? If there's anything else we can do to protect him, I need to know, I need him to be safe."

"You'll have protection, but you'll need to cleanse that area first. There are spirits there that can help you, but only after you've cleared the darkness, so they can see the white light."

"Will they leave after that?" Wade asked.

"No, they cannot leave until we confront the master."

"Who the fuck is the master?" Jimbo yelled, making us all jump.

"You'll soon know, James, but for now you'll need to do as I've directed. Come here when you've finished this task."

After saying our goodbyes, we settled back in the car and drove over to Wade's house. The whole way there I went over all the different ways I knew to protect ourselves; I was willing to try them all after what Janis had told us. I squeezed the rock in my pocket, just knowing it was there made me feel slightly better, but as soon as we were home, we'd be doing the cleansing ceremony. I hoped it actually worked and wasn't one of the many fake ceremonies that produced zero actual results.

"Do we have everything for the cleansing ceremony?" Wade asked.

"I think so, I bought some new smudging sticks that should work great," I said, reaching for his hand. "Jimbo, are you going to join us?"

"Nope, had enough spiritual cleansing to last me five lifetimes. I'm going to head back to Coloma. When you figure out when you're going to meet with Dean again, let me know," he said as we pulled into the driveway.

"I'm going to go work on ordering some promotional

stuff for you guys," Deidre said as she opened the door and stepped out. "See you all later. Bye, James."

He waved to her, and completely ignored us as he walked to his car, got in, and drove off.

"He's such a dick," I said to Wade.

"Yeah, but he's all ours, no one else would put up with his shit," Wade said back.

"You're right, come on, let's get this over with."

"Have you done this before?" Wade asked.

"Only in haunted places, but even then, I never knew if it worked or not. You still have your red jasper, right?"

He felt his pocket. "Yep, right where it should be," he said with a smile.

We walked into the house, and I went to the kitchen to gather the salt, water, bowls, a lighter, and a candle.

"I'll get the smudge stick and be right back," I said, as Wade picked up everything I'd gathered and moved them all to the small table in front of the sofa. When I walked back into the room, he had everything ready to go. I sat on the floor across the table from him. "Are you ready to do this?"

"As ready as I'll ever be. You're sure you know what to do?" he asked.

"I think so." I set everything up like Janis had instructed, and before I lit the candle, I reached across the table and took Wade's hand. He squeezed my hand and took a deep breath and nodded. I lit the candle and then the smudge stick. I blew on it to start it smoking then laid it in an abalone shell. I used a large feather to fan the sage all over Wade. He kept his eyes closed as the smoke enveloped him, waiting patiently while I made sure the smoke had covered every part of him. I then handed him the feather and the bundle of smoking sage, and he did the same to me.

I stood and walked to the back bedroom and smudged every part of the room, repeating this in every room until eventually returning to the living room, where Wade still sat. He watched me as I sat back down across from him, and I took his hand, and another deep breath.

"This ritual will cleanse both of us, all negativity will be gone after we have released it and it has blown away like the smoke on the wind. White light will fill us and leave us both stronger than before, it will protect us. Keep Wade safe from everything evil or any dark forces that would see him harmed. Surround him with white light and keep him safe."

"Jason?"

"Please keep him safe," I finished, and felt a tear slide down my cheek as the flame on the candle died on its own. "It worked, the house is cleansed."

"Jason, I want you to be safe too. I don't want you harmed like you were at The Vineyard House." He moved around the table until he was kneeling next to me on the floor.

"This will keep us both safe, but for some reason these spirits seem to have set their sights on you. And this time we won't let them hurt either of us. We'll listen to what Janis says, and hope she knows what the fuck she's doing. But I won't take any chances with you," I said as I reached out and pulled him into my arms.

"Jason? I can feel you shaking. What's going on?"

"Wade, this is different. There's some force stronger and darker than anything I've ever come across before. I could feel it, when we were in that basement, it's just waiting for someone it can get its claws into and get the hell out of there."

"Do you think it was trapped there by someone?"

"I'm not sure. But we need to go back there and see

what we find. We'll need to be prepared, and not stay there overnight. It's too risky for us all. The longer we're there, the more it'll poke at our defenses, trying to find a weak part, then it'll pounce."

"How do you know this? You've never talked like this before about any of the places we've gone to."

"Something happened at The Vineyard House, I know you felt it too. I'm so aware of the spirits now, I can barely keep them out when I'm anywhere they're at. I have to work on strengthening my defenses. It's like a huge hole was ripped in my consciousness, and all of them know it. They also know you're susceptible to them."

"What do you mean?"

I reached out and cupped his jaw, I couldn't lose him. He wasn't just my best friend; he was the love of my life. We were just starting to explore how close our relationship was. "Wade, you're what they want. Someone who has touched the spirit world and lived to tell about it. You can feel their pain, and they know it. They'll use that to hurt you anytime they're given the opportunity, and as soon as they think you're weak enough, they'll try to take over your body. Only it won't be like the Chalmers, it'll be permanently. The spirits in that basement want help in taking over a body and crossing the veil back to the world of the living." I pulled him close and buried my face in his neck as he wrapped his arms around me and pulled me closer. "I can't lose you, Wade."

He kissed the top of my head before he spoke. "You won't. We'll do everything we can to keep each other safe, but I won't risk you either. We'll both need to be careful, Jimbo too. Did you see the look on his face? He's terrified of whatever we're going to face," Wade said.

"I saw, and he should be terrified. We need to be, and we need to be ready."

"So, what's next?" Wade asked.

"Now we call Dean and see when we can spend some time in that basement. Preferably when it's still light out. At least then they won't have as much power as they will once it's dark."

"Okay then, let's do this." Wade handed me my phone then watched as I dialed, his mouth set in a familiar line of impatience and defiance. I hoped he meant it and he'd be careful, because I knew that if something happened to him, there was no way I'd ever recover.

CHAPTER SEVEN

WADE

I KNEW JASON WAS WORRIED, but I didn't fully understand why. We'd done this so many times, and the only time we'd been in danger was at The Vineyard House. Since then we'd gone to a few small nuisance hauntings, but after we'd cleansed them, there'd been no discernable activity.

I heard him on the phone with Dean, discussing details about when we'd go there. He was very specific in telling him we would not be there after dark. "I realize you may need to close early, but if you want us to check it all out, we cannot be there after dark. It's just too dangerous for us," I heard Jason say. I wasn't sure why it was so important, but I trusted what Jason and Janis had said, and I didn't want to take any chances.

When he ended the call, he walked over to where I was standing in the kitchen. "How'd he take it?" I asked.

"Okay, so at first he wasn't willing to close early, but I explained to him that we wouldn't take the job if he couldn't guarantee we could be there during daylight hours. He agreed we can go in on Wednesday afternoon, they don't have a full booking, so it'll be easy enough for them to close early. He said we could start around five, and he would be willing to stay and make sure we were all safe and accounted for. I'm pretty sure he just wants to see Jimbo again," Jason teased.

"You noticed that too? Jimbo might want to remind him of their time together. The time he conveniently can't remember, but they *maybe* hooked up?" I teased back. "How about if we go practice that hooking up part? I think I might have forgotten what that's all about."

Jason stepped closer to where I stood next to the sink and pressed his body against mine. I would never take this closeness for granted. I rested my hands on his hips and tasted his sweet lips that I never wanted to be without again, and wanted to enjoy as often as was humanly possible. "I think maybe we should go to bed early." I punctuated the suggestion with a kiss. "That way we'll get plenty of sleep, and we'll both be ready to go tomorrow," I added, followed again by multiple kisses. The want and desire for him was always there, but now it was at a point that was hard to ignore—same as his hard dick pressed against my leg.

"If you don't take me to that bed right fucking now—" He left that thought hanging, as he leaned forward and kissed me until we both needed to break away to breathe.

"Bed. Now," was all I managed to get out. Both of us stumbled to the bedroom as we continued to cling to each other with our lips pressed together and our tongues fighting for entrance. We both flopped onto the bed, and I laughed for a second before his mouth was on mine again.

"Why do you still have so many clothes on?" I whispered, as he lifted up enough for us to slip our shirts off. I grazed my thumb across his nipple, causing him to flinch in response before leaning down and kissing me once again. I flipped us over so I was on top, and ground down on his hardness, causing him to groan. He slid his hand into the back of my shorts and cupped my ass.

"Love this ass," he mumbled as he continued to brush his lips down my neck. His breath tickled, and I couldn't hold back the laugh that burst out of me. He gave me a stern look then joined in. We rolled around on the bed, both of us fighting for dominance, neither of us really caring who won. As I slid into him, I was overwhelmed with the feelings I had for him every time we were together: love. I loved him so much it seemed impossible for my heart to contain all the emotions. I brushed my thumb along his cheekbone as I cradled his face and stared into green eyes that reflected those same emotions back at me.

"I love you, Jason, I love you so much," I whispered against his lips.

"I love you too, babe, I've always loved you."

WE CLEANED up and decided it was probably time to make something for dinner. We spent most evenings together, but deep inside I hoped we'd end up living together.

"What are you thinking about?" he asked, smoothing the lines between my brows.

"Just you, always you, Jason." He kissed me again, and we both settled in to decide what to do for dinner—cook or order in. His phone sounded with the familiar sound of Jimbo's ringtone; the "Imperial March" was so perfect for him, it made me laugh every time he called.

"Hey, Jimbo, what's going on?" Jason greeted him. "I'm putting you on speaker so Wade can hear you."

"Whatever, asshole," Jimbo mumbled.

"Watch your language, you don't want Wade's mama giving you a smackdown for your rude talk," Jason admonished playfully.

"Yeah, yeah, whatever—asshole."

"What did you want? Or are you just calling to give me crap?"

"Fuck you, Jason, I called to see when we're going to Dean's place?" Jason and I made eye contact, and both of us struggled for some control before he answered.

"We're going Wednesday afternoon, if you want to go, be here around four. That should give us plenty of time to get there and be ready as soon as the place closes," Jason said.

"Yeah, okay, I'll be there. You explained to him about not being there after dark?" Jimbo asked, a tinge of uncertainty in his tone.

"Yes, I'm not sure he completely understands, but he was willing to go along with it. I think he wants this all to be over with, and he knows what he's been doing has done nothing to stop the activity they keep having," Jason said.

"I don't think he realizes how serious it is, this is as bad, if not worse, than what we experienced in Coloma. And he has no clue about any of that beyond what was online or on TV," I added.

"He never believed anything like that was real. I tried to talk to him when he worked there, but he brushed it off, until shit got real uncomfortable for everyone there. I don't know how much longer he stayed after I left. But once I got a good look at old man Chalmers, that was more than enough for me," Jimbo mumbled, still not completely comfortable discussing the events he'd witnessed there.

"If things go as bad as we're expecting, I think he won't

have any choice but to believe. His place is just waking up, once it gets started there, it's going to be hard to stop. And none of his employees will be safe going down in that basement, alone or otherwise," Jason said. "And wait, Dean worked at The Vineyard House?"

Jimbo ignored the question with a grunt, so we said our goodbyes, and he agreed to meet us here, and we'd drive over together.

I turned to Jason, just as he was turning to me, and we both smiled at how in tune we were to each other. "Want to start packing our kit for Wednesday? I know it's only Sunday, but we'll need to gather a few items we won't want to go in without, for protection," Jason said.

"That sounds great, but for now, let's eat, and get back to bed. I want to feel you wrapped around me one more time tonight." His eyes smoldered as I glanced over my shoulder at him while walking into the living room.

"You can't just say that and walk away," he joked as he tackled me to the couch, and we forgot about food for a second time that day.

CHAPTER EIGHT

JASON

I'D SPENT the last two days researching any way to protect us from whatever the fuck was in that basement. Janis had mentioned "the master," but I had found no mention online or in any of the reference books I had at home. I called Jimbo while Wade was at work, and asked him what he thought it was, but he had no idea either. He explained that Janis was connected to the spirit world in ways he didn't understand, and he didn't want to. He admitted it scared the fuck out of him, which did nothing to relieve the anxiety I felt clawing at me as we prepared to drive over to The Hitching Post.

Jimbo walked into the house after parking in the driveway. "Hey, make yourself at home," I called out to him.

"Oh I will, thank you very much," he said, before walking into the kitchen and rummaging around in the refrigerator.

"And help yourself to anything you want," I said, rolling my eyes. Wade shoved past me and walked into the kitchen.

"Hey, Jimbo, you ready for today?" he asked. Jimbo froze, head in the refrigerator and his ass sticking out of the half-open door. He stepped back and closed the door, juggling the soda and leftover Chinese food container he held in his hands.

"I'm as ready as I'll ever be. I didn't get a chance to eat when I was at work. I went in early and had to clean the fryer before I left. That's never a good experience."

"Uh, okay. Help yourself, we need to leave here soon, though, so we're not late. I'm hoping Dean can close a little earlier and give us a little more time. As it is, we'll only get a few hours," I said.

"Let's hit it, I can eat on the way," Jimbo announced, then walked back out the door he'd just come in. Wade started to follow him, but I hooked his elbow before he got too far.

"Jason? Did you forget something?" I stood for a moment and looked at him, not wanting to ever forget what he looked like in that moment, his eyes full of excitement and expectation. His hair was slightly longer than he normally wore it, reminding me of how he'd looked when we were kids. Board shorts hung low on his hips, and his T-shirt was just tight enough to show off how lean he was, but not so tight it looked like he was trying to show it off. I loved him, probably more than I'd ever loved anyone. And I'd fight anything or anyone that tried to take him away from me.

"No, I didn't forget anything. Just enjoying the view, that's all." He stepped close to me and captured my lips in a quick kiss, then pulled me in for a warm hug.

"Come on, let's get this over with so we can get back here and figure out what the hell is going on there." I nodded and followed him out the door to the car.

"I'm driving," I said as I brushed past Wade. He walked around and got in the passenger side. "I'm hoping everything goes smooth while we're there. I don't want to start out this job having it all go to shit."

"I checked everything, we should be good to go," Wade said.

I looked in the mirror to see Jimbo eating like he didn't have a care in the world. We drove down the freeway until we took the exit for Old Sacramento, and since it was midweek, we had no problem finding a parking space. When we walked up to the door for The Hitching Post, Dean met us.

"I'm so glad you guys are here, I'm not sure what's changed, but there's been a lot of activity the past few days."

"What's happened?" I asked. We all walked in and sat at a table while we waited for Dean to speak.

"I'm not sure how to describe it, but there is just this heaviness here. My whole staff has been on edge, and no one can go into the basement. Anytime we've tried, the door won't open. Or if we get it open it slams shut again. After a few times of that, no one was willing to keep trying," he said as he brushed two fingers along his forehead.

"Are you okay?" Jimbo asked. Dean looked up in surprise, I knew how he felt. Jimbo rarely showed any worry for anyone other than Wade's mom.

"Yeah, why wouldn't I be?"

"Have you gone down there since we were here last?" Wade asked.

"No, I made sure the staff never went alone, and we haven't had any problems until the past few days—it's been worse than ever. I can't run a business like this. I mean, we could move the storage room upstairs, but that takes time, and we'd need to clear an area up here for it. It's just more time that we don't have."

"Let's get started. Wade, you take the EMF, Jimbo,

bring that bag that has the flashlights and the supplies we need to cleanse the area. I'll bring the Flir camera and the recorder. I want us to be upstairs before the sun goes down. Dean, did you want to go with us?" I asked.

"I'm not sure," he answered.

"You're welcome to accompany us, but we'll need to cleanse your aura first. That way you won't be as vulnerable to the spirits that may be there," I explained to him.

"I think I'll pass. This isn't really my thing. I'll wait up here for you guys, and if you're not back here by the time it's dark out, I'll call someone for help."

"Basements aren't really my thing either," Wade mumbled, and looked at the door.

"That's probably a good idea. Here, let me give you Jimbo's sister's number. If anything happens, call her and Wade's mom, here's her number too. They'll know what to do," I instructed, as I found both numbers and sent them to him in a text. "You guys ready?"

"Let's go," Wade said, and moved toward the basement door like he hadn't said a word.

"Fuck," Jimbo said, and dragged his feet, following Wade.

"Dean, give us two hours, if we're not back by then, bring in the reinforcements."

"You got it. Good luck, and be careful." I nodded and walked past Wade so I was the first one down the stairs. Dean was right, something had changed; it felt different this time than the last, heavier, and more foreboding.

"Do you feel that?" Wade whispered from behind me as he clutched the back of my shirt.

"I feel it, there's more of them here now. It's like something is rounding them up and bringing them to this area. Jimbo, you've got your power locked down, right?"

41

"Are you kidding me? There is no way in hell I'm opening myself up to this shit."

"Okay, just checking, here we go. And remember, Wade, don't take any chances." He nodded at me and clenched my shirt even tighter. I turned and opened the door. It swung open easily. The light was on, and it looked the same as it had last week, random items neatly stored. Nothing weird to make me think we were in any danger. I stepped into the room, with Wade right behind me, followed by Jimbo.

"Something's not right," I whispered. The energy in the room started to crackle, as though it was building up for something. I reached back to reassure myself Wade was still close as I walked into the back part of the room, where I'd sensed the spirits the last time we'd been here. I tried opening myself up to their presence, trying to gauge how many there were, and if they meant us harm. Before I could sense anything, the door slammed shut. We all turned at the same time, startled by the sudden noise, and all froze for a second before the lights flicked off and we were drowned in a darkness so black I couldn't tell if my eyes were open or closed.

"Jimbo, are you okay?" Wade asked.

"Yes, but I'm not fucking moving when I can't see shit," Jimbo whisper-yelled.

"Can you get a flashlight out of the bag?" I asked.

"Oh yeah, man, sorry, give me a second." I heard him scrambling around, digging in a bag, and then a scraping sound at the opposite side of the room from us. I realized with a start, I couldn't feel Wade any longer.

"Wade? Don't move until we have some light in here," I said, but he didn't answer. Jimbo lit a flashlight, and the beam hit me straight in the eyes, blinding me temporarily.

"Sorry, I couldn't see where you were," he said as he moved the beam to look around the area—and froze. "Where's Wade?" he asked.

I spun around. While there were crates and shelves filling the room, this wasn't such a big space that he could hide and go undetected. "Wade?" I asked. Looking around again, I tried to make some sense of where Wade was.

"Where is he?" Jimbo asked again.

"I'm not sure, he was right behind me, how the fuck can we not see him? There's no place for him to hide." Then we heard it, a scraping sound, outside the basement and in the larger space that made up the underground area. I rushed over to Jimbo and took the flashlight from him and swung it toward the noise. Wade was out there without a light, and in complete darkness.

"Wade, don't move. Wait until I can get to you with a flashlight." I was near panic as I rushed to get to him. I crossed the barrier into the larger area, and as I got closer, Wade turned to look at me. His eyes reflected fear so intense it froze me in place, and then he was gone.

CHAPTER NINE

WADE

"WHAT HAPPENED?" I said, mostly to myself. One minute I was standing in the pitch-black basement, waiting for Jimbo to hand me a flashlight, then I saw a flash of movement outside of the basement area. I went through the barrier that was meant to keep the two areas separate, and ended up in an even darker area, stumbling on uneven ground. I tried to go back the way I'd come, but it was so completely dark I couldn't tell exactly which direction that was.

I turned to see where Jason was, and as our eyes locked, a jolt of fear hit me when I realized what was about to happen. There was a scraping sound to my right, and out of the corner of my eye I caught another flash of movement, then the ground seemed to disappear under my feet. I had no time to react before I fell down into a hole. Hitting rocks and what felt like wooden beams all the way to the bottom, I landed with a splash in a few inches of water. For a few seconds I couldn't breathe. My chest burned, and I wondered if I'd broken ribs, or something else, then in a sudden whoosh, I was able to draw in a much-needed breath.

Coughing and sputtering, I struggled to fill my lungs, the air was damp and smelled of dirt and mildew. I blinked, trying to see any detail of where I was, but it was so dark I couldn't see anything. I rolled to my side and felt my pocket for my phone and pulled it out. I fumbled with it, and finally got it to light up. Shining it around, I realized I was in a cave, or maybe a mineshaft. I knew there were many rumored to be all around this area, but I'd never seen one, let alone fallen into one. I sat in the water and shined the light around. I couldn't see the top of the shaft, but it was a pitch black hole in the area I'd fallen from, so I had no reference to tell how far it actually was.

I brushed at my hair, and flinched as pain shot through me. My fingers touched a wet and sticky substance and its faint coppery scent made me realize I had blood running from a cut on my head. I swallowed hard to force down the urge to vomit. I had to concentrate on finding a way out of here. I sat still and listened for a second, all I could hear was the trickle of water and more of the complete silence we'd heard in the basement.

Jason, oh god, he'd be freaking out. I cupped my hands as I yelled up the shaft, "Jason! I'm here, can you hear me?" I strained to hear, but still only heard the faint trickle of water. I shined my phone light around, hoping to find a way to climb out, but there was nothing—the walls were far too smooth for me to be able to climb out on my own.

I held my phone up and checked for a signal, but there was none. "Fuck!" I yelled, and instantly regretted it as my head pounded and blood now ran into my eye. I wiped it away and clenched my hand. What the fuck was I going to do? I couldn't go up, and I couldn't just sit here and wait until Jason and Jimbo found me. I needed to get out of here as soon as possible.

I shined the light around the space again and noticed an area that went back deeper into a tunnel from the space I was in. My light didn't penetrate far, and I wasn't sure it was a good idea to go wandering around in an underground cave or mineshaft that probably wasn't on any map. I reached my hand in my pocket, checking to see if I'd brought anything with me that could help. I took out the EMF detector and turned it on. At first there was nothing, then slowly it started to spike. I froze. There was nowhere for me to go, I had nowhere to hide, and nothing to protect myself with.

Suddenly I could feel it; something was down here with me. I swung my light around again, hoping to catch a glimpse of whatever it was before it made its presence known. The dark seemed to get even darker, and it now had a weight to it. The urge to crouch down and clasp my arms over my head to protect myself from whatever was down here was so strong I fought to ignore it, too afraid to give it an advantage over me.

"H—hello? Is someone there?" I called, fearful there would be a response, and terrified of what it might be. I heard a scraping sound, deep in the tunnel beyond what my light could reach. I backed up to the wall and pressed back against it as flat as I could. My breath started to come in shallow gasps, and I couldn't control the shivers that seemed to rack my whole body. The scraping slowly moved closer to me, but still I couldn't see anything. Cold dread coursed through my blood as I fought to not scream. Fear took over and I spun away from the sound, my hands clawed at the dirt and stone walls, hoping to somehow be able to climb out.

Suddenly there was a bright light that flashed right behind me. I shielded my eyes from it as I slowly turned around while trying to make out what happened. A little girl stood before me, dressed as though she was from the 1800s, her hair in two long braids. The same girl we'd seen at The Vineyard House. And I now realized, in the haunted house we'd visited for Halloween.

"You need to leave here, I can only distract him for a short time," she said, looking straight at me before glancing behind her into the dark void.

"Who? What's down there?" I asked, trying like hell not to panic and doing a shitty job of it. She looked at me again and took a step in my direction.

"You know what it is, you've been warned about this, and you should have taken heed and been more careful."

"Where's Jason, is he okay?" I asked, frantic that somehow Jason was in more trouble than I was.

"Wade, you need to leave this place at once, I can only hold him off temporarily," she said, before turning and running into the dark. As soon as she passed the darkest point, I could no longer see her. Fuck it, I was getting the hell out of here. I wedged my back against one side and braced my legs and hands on the other side. Slowly I started to inch my way up to the surface. I tried not to look down, knowing I would only see a dark hole. Whatever was down there was now closer, and if I fell, there was no way I was getting out of here in one piece. It seemed to take forever, but was probably actually just a few minutes, until I was nearly at the top.

"Wade," I heard Jason calling from somewhere just above the top of the hole.

"Jason, down here, be careful, there's an opening to a mine," I yelled as I shimmied closer to the top. I heard footfalls on the dirt floor, and finally saw Jason and Jimbo poke their heads over the edge to peer down at me.

"Wade," Jason yelled, panic clear in his voice. "Are you hurt?" I could tell he was trying to stay calm, but he was near his limit. When he reached down, I was close enough to grip his hand.

"Pull me up, get me the fuck out of here." My heart pounded, and I could feel the panic rising up in me again. Jason and Jimbo both pulled at once, and we all landed in a heap on the dirt floor. Jason scrambled over to me and pulled me into his arms.

"Are you okay? You were gone, we were in the basement and suddenly you were gone. Are you hurt? Oh god, you're bleeding and you're soaking wet," Jason said as he tried to check for injuries, at the same time holding me close. I clung to him, and the shivering I'd had now became severe shaking.

"We need to get you out of here. Let's get you upstairs so we can make sure you don't need a doctor." He slipped his arm around my back and helped me along to the door. I tried the lights and they came on, illuminating the area that had not changed since we'd entered it. Jimbo turned the doorknob and it opened right up. We climbed the stairs, and Dean sat at the nearest table to the basement door. He looked up from the paperwork he had laid out in front of him, unable to cover his shocked expression as we emerged.

"What happened?" he asked, rushing over to us.

"Fucking ghosts, that's what happened," Jimbo said. Jason and I looked at each other, and he pulled out a chair for me to sit.

"We need more help than magic stones," I said to Jason, but Jimbo was the one who slumped into the chair next to me.

"I was afraid of that," he said.

CHAPTER TEN

JASON

I RUSHED OVER to Wade as soon as I heard him calling, my eyes wide with fear when I realized he was down in what looked like an old mineshaft. He struggled to climb all the way to the top, but it was obvious he was too exhausted to make it. Jimbo and I both gripped his hands and tugged him over the edge. Without thinking, I pulled him to me and held him, probably too tight, but not nearly tight enough.

"I thought I'd lost you," I whispered into his ear, not even sure he'd heard me. I started rambling, asking if he was injured and what had happened to him, as he trembled from fear or being wet, I wasn't sure which. He ducked his head and leaned against my chest. He seemed so lost and vulnerable in that moment, and Wade never seemed vulnerable. I looped my arm around his back to help him upstairs, as Jimbo took his other side. Jimbo's arm shook so badly, I could feel it where our arms met on Wade's back. We hurried to get him to the top of the stairs, something made much easier with the lights on.

When we burst out of the door, Dean looked up in

shock. He pulled out a chair for Wade, then rushed to get some water and towels to clean him up. "Are you sure you're okay? I think we should get you checked out. How far did you fall?"

"I'm not sure," Wade said, then closed his eyes and gritted his teeth. There was blood trickling down his cheek from his forehead, and he was covered in dirt and grime. I moved his hair and tried to get a good look at the wound. He flinched away from me and folded his arms across his stomach as he continued to shake.

"Baby, I think we need to take you to the hospital, that cut looks like it needs stitches. And I'm pretty sure you're close to going into shock." I tried to stay calm, but I knew he needed more help than we could give him. Dean returned with towels and a bottle of water, which I handed to Wade. He drank it down, some of the water dribbling down his front, but he didn't even seem to notice. I used one of the towels and dabbed at his face; he still had not met my eyes, and he continued to shake like a leaf.

"I think you need to take him to a hospital, and soon, before he goes into shock," Dean said, giving Wade a worried look. Jimbo sat to the side, looking confused and stressed.

"I think you're right. Jimbo, can you go get the car and pull up close to the door?" I said as I dug my keys out and handed them to him. He ran out the door as I turned back to Wade. He still hadn't said much, and the haunted look in his eyes didn't make me feel any better about his mental state. "Babe, are you okay?" I asked, pouring water onto a towel and wiping gently at his face. He had mud smeared everywhere and was wet. He didn't feel cold to the touch, but he still shivered uncontrollably. I took his hand in mine and shook it, frantic to have him react to me.

Suddenly his eyes shot to mine, and he jerked his hand away from me at the same time. He scrambled to put more space between us and pushed the chair he sat in back across the floor. He only made it a short distance before it flipped over. As soon as he hit the floor he was on his hands and knees, trying to clamber away. "Wade," I shouted as I moved toward him. Dean stepped in front of me and rushed over to where Wade still tried to put more distance between us, until he hit the wall and curled into a ball. I moved to go to him, but Dean held his hand up, stopping me in my tracks. He knelt down and gently placed his hand on Wade's back, causing him to flinch.

"Wade? Are you okay? Jason and I want to take you to the hospital, would that be all right?" Dean asked.

Wade slowly uncurled his arms and looked straight at Dean. Blood ran freely from the cut on his head, and he sweated profusely, while his breath came in harsh pants.

"Get the fuck away from me," he yelled, before he seemed to crumple onto the wooden floor.

"Wade!" I hurried over to his side. He was limp and didn't react at all as I pulled him into my arms. "Wade, please wake up," I whispered into his hair. I felt him move and pulled back enough to see his face.

"Jason? We need to get out of here, we did it all wrong. Fuck, we did it all wrong."

"I know, I know. Jimbo went to get the car, we're taking you to the hospital," I said, simultaneously filled with shock and relief that he was talking and knew who I was.

"We can't go down there alone again, Dean has to go, and we have to do everything exactly like Janis told us to. We were so stupid." He brushed his fingers along his forehead, and his eyes grew wide when he noticed blood on his fingertips.

"Dean, give me that towel," I yelled in a panic. He rushed to the table we'd been seated at and brought the towels and bottled water. He didn't ask, just started pressing the towel to Wade's head. Jimbo burst in through the door, eyes wide with shock. He froze for a second before he knelt in front of Wade.

"Wade, dude, we're going to get you to a hospital, okay?"

"Thanks, Jimbo, I think that's a good idea." Jimbo reached for Wade, but I hurried to help him stand; he swayed slightly on his feet, and Jimbo rushed to the other side to help.

"Let me get the door." Dean opened it and watched as we hurried past him. "Call me and let me know how Wade is," he called out as we crossed the sidewalk to the car that was now parked right in front of the restaurant.

"I will. Thanks for helping. And Dean—" I helped Wade into the back seat. "—don't let anyone go into that basement. No one!" I yelled back over my shoulder.

"I understand, I'll wait to hear from you."

I nodded and slid into the seat next to Wade. There was no way I wasn't sitting right next to him. I gathered him up and pulled him into my side, kissing the side of his head.

"Jimbo, hurry the fuck up." He slid behind the wheel and hit the gas. "We fucked up, Jimbo."

"I know, Jason, but we can still fix it." I hoped like hell he was right, and I hoped Wade could forgive me for putting him in danger.

CHAPTER ELEVEN

WADE

I REMEMBERED CLIMBING out of that fucking hole, but then everything seemed to get hazy. I knew Jason and Jimbo helped me out, and rushed me up the stairs, but once I was there I couldn't stop shaking. My head felt like it would split in half, and I couldn't seem to stop the thoughts and sounds that rushed through my mind. We'd done everything wrong. When we'd gotten here, we'd been so anxious to see what would happen, we ignored what Janis had explicitly told us to do.

"Jason, we can't take any more chances. We have to do everything right from now on," I said, turning to meet his eyes.

"I know, I can't believe I was so stupid, I'm so sorry I put you in danger. I—"

"We're both guilty, we both knew what we were supposed to do, and we didn't do it." I knew he'd try to blame himself; even through the buzzing in my head I could hear his guilt.

"We'll be there in just a few minutes," Jimbo said from the front seat. I wasn't sure how long we'd been in the car, but it couldn't have been long. It felt like a few seconds passed and he was pulling up to the emergency entrance of the closest hospital. It was still a little light out, but the bright lights of the entrance caused me to recoil in pain as Jason opened my car door to help me out.

"I'll park the car and meet you guys in there," Jimbo said, as Jason led me to the doors.

We ended up waiting for a couple of hours. Most of it I slept through, drifting in and out of consciousness, only slightly aware of the dull ache in my side, while Jason and Jimbo sat on either side of me. When they finally called my name, Jason kept his arm around me and helped me stand.

"Sorry, sir, you can't go back with him," the admissions nurse said.

"I'm his boyfriend, and I'm not leaving him," Jason said. She nodded without arguing further and led us back to a bed that was surrounded by curtains. Jason helped me to the bed, and I let myself relax on it until the doctor came to examine me.

"Mr. Rivers, I haven't seen you for a few years," the doctor said as he entered.

"Oh, hey, Doc Evans, long time no see," Jason said as he held out his hand to shake the doctor's hand.

"Please tell me you guys have given up the ghost hunting?" he said as he stepped closer and started cleaning my forehead.

"Ouch, watch it, Doc."

"So, what happened this time?"

"I fell down into an old mineshaft, I'm pretty sure I landed on my head," I explained.

"Did you lose consciousness?" he asked, still dabbing at my forehead.

"Not that I remember. I landed on my side pretty hard,

though, and hit a few rocks on the way down." He helped me take my shirt off, and Jason took in a shocked breath. "I think you might have cracked a rib here, we'll need to do a few X-rays, just to be sure."

We ended up spending a few hours there. When I was finally released around midnight, Doc Evans said I had a slight concussion and bruised ribs. He glued the cut on my forehead closed and made me promise not to fall headfirst in any more holes in the near future. We pulled up to my house around one, and I could barely keep my eyes open.

"Come on, baby, let's get you to bed," Jason said, practically carrying me into the house. "Jimbo, you're welcome to stay, it's late for you to drive all that way back to Coloma."

"All right, thanks, man. I'm beat, I'll probably just sleep a couple of hours then head back in time for the breakfast rush."

"Sounds good," Jason said, and led me to the bedroom. He set me gently on the bed and knelt to take my shoes off. Much as I had taken care of him, now he took care of me. I smiled down at him as I struggled to stay awake.

"Go ahead and lay back, I've got you," he said, smoothing my hair back from the bandage that now covered my forehead.

When I woke up again, it was dark out, Jason held me close, and his even breaths comforted me and made me feel even more at ease. But then I remembered what had happened, and I noticed my phone light up. I moved to pick it up, and the pain in my side reminded me of my injury. Looking at my phone, I squinted at the bright screen, and saw a text from Janis.

Wade I told you it would only work if you did exactly what I said to do. You need to go back, as soon as you can and do it right.

I read it a few times before tapping out an answer. We'd go back, and this time be more prepared and do everything exactly like she'd told us to. No more fucking around. This time we'd be ready.

I know, we really fucked up.

Call me tomorrow and give me all the details, we'll go over again what you guys need to do. But the longer you wait the worse it will be.

Okay, I'll call. Thanks Janis.

"Who's that?" Jason asked as he propped up his head on his hand.

"Janis. I'm sorry I woke you up."

"You didn't, are you feeling better?"

"Yeah, my headache is only a slight roar now. Jason, thanks for getting me out of there. I couldn't have done it without you and Jimbo."

He reached for me with his other hand and settled for taking my hand and resting it on the bed between us. "I was so worried about you," he whispered, leaning closer to me.

"I'm sorry, I didn't mean any of it to happen. I thought I saw something and followed it out there to get a closer look. As soon as I started to fall, I knew I'd screwed up."

"Shh, don't. We all fucked up, we knew exactly what we needed to do, and we didn't do it. I'm so glad you weren't hurt any worse than you were," Jason said.

"We can't wait to go back; Janis said the longer we wait, the harder it's going to be. Can you call Dean tomorrow and see when he's able to make time for us again?" He gave me a hard look for a moment before answering.

"Are you sure? We don't have to go back. We can

contact another ghost-hunting group and see if they can take over."

"Jason, you know we need to do this. But we need to do it right. Janis tried to prepare us, and none of us took it serious enough to make sure we followed her instructions."

"I know you're right, but I can't stand the idea of you being in danger. What if you'd hurt yourself even worse when you fell? You could have broken a bone and not been able to climb out. Or you could have been knocked unconscious and we wouldn't have been able to find you until who knew when."

I could feel the panic starting to rise in him. He'd been strong for me at the hospital, but he was scared for me. Something I understood after what had happened at The Vineyard House. "I won't take any chances again. I didn't even think about walking out there. I knew from when we'd been there before it was smooth and flat out there, and there weren't any obstacles. I never even thought about there being an old mineshaft." I shook my head and winced.

"Hey, there was no way you could have known about it. Let's get some sleep and we'll figure it all out tomorrow. I'll call Dean and see when he has time again. I love you, Wade, and I'm so damn glad you're okay." He gently kissed the top of my head, and I lay my head on his chest. My last thought was how much I loved him too, and how much our lives had changed. I'd fight for him, no matter who or what stood in the way. We'd survived The Vineyard House, and we'd survive this too.

CHAPTER TWELVE

JASON

I WOKE up before Wade and let him sleep. He was reluctant to admit how badly he was hurt, and I tried like hell not to keep thinking about it. I used the bathroom and walked out into the living room; the sun was barely beginning to rise, and Jimbo was just pulling his shoes on.

"You out of here?" I asked.

"Yeah, I'll give you a call later on. I need to work this morning and do a few things around the restaurant," Jimbo said as he moved to the door. "Take care of him, I know he doesn't want to acknowledge how bad he was hurt, but . . . well, you know . . ." He rubbed the back of his neck as he looked down at the floor, seeming unsure of what he wanted to say.

"I'll take care of him, don't worry. We won't be stupid this time," I said.

"This time? What are you saying?"

"We have to go back, Janis said we shouldn't wait. I'm going to call Dean this morning and see when we can return."

He moved closer to me and lowered his voice. "Jason, he

could have been killed. I didn't want to say it, but you know it's true. It seems like everything we do makes the next ordeal that much worse."

"We'll be careful, I won't let him be hurt again."

He looked directly into my eyes, and after a few seconds, he nodded. "I know you'll take care of him, but we need to listen next time. And do exactly what Janis says. I've fought her advice my whole life, and looking back, if I'd just listened to her, I could have saved myself a shitload of trouble. She warned me about The Vineyard House. The day after I took the job, she showed up at my door, told me it was a mistake, to stay away or I'd find out how real the other side was. I laughed at her, told her to sell it to someone else. I knew weird things happened around the two of us, but I didn't want to admit what it really was."

"Hey, I get it. I knew how uncomfortable Wade was with the supernatural. I still made him go with me to play ghost hunter."

"You didn't make me do anything, I went because I loved you," Wade said from the bedroom door as he slowly started toward me.

"Let me help you," I said, rushing to his side to help him sit on the couch.

"Thanks, I'm really feeling it this morning," Wade said, brushing his lips against mine.

"And with that, I'm off to work. Talk to you guys later," Jimbo said, then practically ran out the door.

"What can I get you?" I asked Wade, watching as he gingerly moved around, trying to find a comfortable position, but he ignored my question. "Nothing? Okay, I'll just get your phone." When I walked back out, his eyes were shut as he relaxed back on the couch. I started to leave his phone next to him, and he grabbed my arm, startling me.

"Don't forget to call Dean, we need to finish this."

"I'll do it right now." He settled back on the couch and seemed ready to fall right back to sleep. Not wanting to put it off any longer, I dialed Dean. "Hey, Dean, this is Jason, just calling to see when it's a good time to come back again."

"Hello, Jason, is Wade okay?" Dean immediately asked.

"Yeah, we took him to the ER, and he has a slight concussion and bruised ribs. Bad enough, but not anything serious. Sorry I didn't call you sooner," I added.

"That's okay, I'm just relived to know he wasn't injured worse than he was. Jason, I need to ask you something, and I want you to be honest. Do you think I'm asking too much? Is the situation at the restaurant more serious than any of us thought?" he asked.

I paused for a moment to collect my thoughts before I answered. "I know this all seems crazy, but we've dealt with much worse. I know you're aware of what was going on at The Vineyard House, and honestly, this is pretty bad. But at least we're not stuck in the middle of nowhere, with no one to call for help if we need it. We just need to refocus our efforts and do exactly what Jimbo's sister told us to do. None of us did that, we all rushed in blindly," I said, and glanced over to where Wade seemed to have fallen back to sleep.

"I'm not sure there's a right and wrong way to do it. I think the spirits that seem to be under the restaurant are very powerful. The Vineyard House was terrifying, I hated working there. But this is on a whole different level. I keep thinking about how lucky Wade was to not have been injured more than he was," Dean said.

"I hate that he was injured, and I can't help but blame myself. I know more about the supernatural than he or Jimbo. But Jimbo's sister gave us specific instructions on how to proceed safely, and we were so ready to get in there, we didn't do it. There's a few things you need to know before you commit to having us return," I said earnestly.

"Okay, go ahead."

"First, we'll need to do a spiritual cleansing on you and the restaurant."

"Is this something I'll need to prepare for? Or will you be able to plan for everything?" he asked.

"We'll bring everything, it's mostly burning sage and other herbs to force out any bad entities that may want to make it harder for us to convince them all to leave."

"What else?" Dean asked. So far, he was taking this all amazingly well.

"You'll need to go with us into the basement. I think—"

"Fuck that," he said before I could finish.

"Excuse me?"

"I'm not going down there. I haven't been down there since you guys first came and you said there were multiple spirits."

"Dean, you have to. Without you, it can't be done. I'm not sure what's waiting for us down there, but I know it's not good. And believe me, if we could do it without your help, we would. Hell, if I could do it without putting Wade in danger I would. But we have specific instructions, and we've seen how it works out when we don't follow them. I don't want to unleash something else even more powerful." When he was silent for a few seconds, I pulled my phone from my ear and looked at it, thinking he must have hung up.

"I'll close the place tonight, can you do it then? If I wait any longer, I'll back out. Do it as soon as you can, Jason."

"We'll be there. Let me talk to Wade and Jimbo and see what time we can all be there. And Dean, we need to do it before dark, I can't stress that enough." He hung up, and I met Wade's worried gaze.

"What did he say?" he asked, struggling to sit up. I pulled him close and told him everything, and without even asking, I knew he'd be ready to go whenever I asked him to.

CHAPTER THIRTEEN

WADE

I LISTENED as Jason told me everything he'd talked to Dean about. I wasn't sure I'd be physically ready so soon, but I knew if we waited any longer to begin, we'd have no chance of succeeding. I could tell by the urgency in his voice he knew it too.

"Call Jimbo, if he can be here today, we need to do this. Let's make it clear to those assholes that we're not afraid of them, and we have some tricks up our sleeve too. There's a few of your toys you need to bring," I said, and flinched when I tried to get up off the couch.

"Let me help you," Jason said, and very gently helped me to my feet.

"Thanks, I feel like I got hit by a truck." He stopped and turned to face me, looking at me as though he was checking I wasn't injured more. Ducking his head, he very carefully wrapped me in his arms and pulled me close. "Don't worry, it'll all be better this time, I can feel it."

"I won't ever forgive myself for you getting hurt, I still can't believe you fell down into a mineshaft."

"Jason, you got hurt when I was watching out for you. I

know how easy it is for shit to happen. You didn't hurt me, and you didn't let me be hurt. It just happened. And we won't let it happen again," I said into his hair as I tried to hold him tight to me without causing myself intense pain.

"We'll look out for each other, we'll slow down and make sure we do everything right," Jason said.

"That sounds perfect. How about we call Jimbo and make sure he can go later. If he can't, we'll need to reschedule." We walked into the kitchen, and Jason set his phone on the counter, dialed Jimbo, and put it on speakerphone.

"What the fuck do you want, Jason? I'm busy," Jimbo snapped, no greeting—his usual.

"Hey, Jimbo, we talked to Dean and he said we could go back today. I wanted to check if that's good for you?"

"Fuck," Jimbo mumbled. It sounded like he set his phone down for a second, and the sounds of him cooking and barking out orders were loud and clear through the line.

"Well, can you make it?" Jason asked.

"Yes, I don't like it, but what else can I do?"

"Thanks, man, don't forget to bring your stone," I reminded him.

"I always carry it, I'm not risking it," he replied.

"I'll tell Dean today works, if you can get down here early, that's even better. I don't want to be in the basement after dark," Jason said.

"No shit, I'll be there as soon as I can get someone to cover me for lunch."

"Thanks, Jimbo, see you soon," I said, and he hung up without another word. I called my work and let them know I'd be taking the next couple of days off. After I explained to them I was injured, they were more than happy to give me the time off. Hopefully by Monday I'd be ready to go back.

"Wade, can I ask you something?" Jason started, seeming very unsure of whatever it was he wanted to ask.

"Anything, what is it?"

"What did you see down there?"

"I'm not sure, I know what I think it was, but I'm not sure if that's right or not."

"What?"

"When I was down there, something else was in there with me. I couldn't see it, but I could feel it, and the EMF detected it. But before it found me, someone else did."

"What do you mean?" Jason asked.

"Remember the little girl we filmed on the stairs at The Vineyard House?"

"With the long braids? Yes."

"She was there, she told me I needed to get out of there before 'he' got there. That she'd keep him busy so I'd have time to get out."

Jason gave me a shocked look before he responded, "She helped you get out?"

"She kept whatever is down there busy so I had a chance to climb out."

"What do you think it is?"

"I'm not sure, but it was dark, not only in color, but the way it felt. It felt like it sucked all the light out of the area and was ready to draw anything out of me it could get to."

"Like a vampire?" Jason asked.

"Maybe, I'm not sure, I just knew I didn't want to be down there with it."

"I think we should both do another spiritual cleansing here, right now. When we get to Dean's we'll do it again. But I'm not taking any chances, we'll clear our auras of any negativity, then fill up on some good energy before we go. We'll have our stones, so that'll help too."

"I knew you'd know what to do, now let's get going on preparing for later," I said, while I hoped, deep inside, we really were ready this time.

CHAPTER FOURTEEN

JASON

WADE FELL ASLEEP AGAIN, not long after we'd talked. I took the opportunity to gather the ovilus and a spirit box to take with us. We didn't normally use these because they were very loud, and so far the places we'd gone to hadn't wanted it to be made public that we were there investigating. I hoped they might help us get some insight into what was haunting Dean's restaurant, and why it was still there. I picked up the stone that had been chosen for me: black tourmaline. I hoped Janis was right and it helped protect me.

I gathered everything I'd need to cleanse the house and started in the back bedroom. I carried the smoking bundle of herbs in an abalone shell and fanned it around the room with a feather, making sure the smoke went everywhere. When I made my way to the living room, Wade was awake and sitting up. He watched me as I wafted the smoke around the room, and as I opened the front door and wafted some out, hoping anything bad followed it outside.

"We'll need to do a spiritual cleansing, hopefully it works. I keep thinking about Janis saying we would be infected by any spirits we may encounter. Where's your stone?" I asked.

Wade felt for his pocket. "It's in my pants pocket. I put it in there before we left."

"At least you remembered, I can't believe I forgot. I'll get it for you." I walked into the bedroom and picked up the shorts he'd had on yesterday, they were blood-stained, muddy, and wet. I dug in his pocket and found his stone tucked in his right front pocket.

"Here you go, it was right where it should have been. Do you think these stones are strong enough to really protect us?"

"I'm not sure, I don't know much about using stones for protection, but I trust what Janis says. She knows what she's doing, and she wouldn't tell us to do something just to mess with us. I think we had problems because we did exactly what she said not to do," Wade said as he reached for his stone.

"Red jasper, did you look it up to see what it protects from?" I asked.

"No, did you look up yours?"

"No, let's check it out, maybe there's something else we can do to make it stronger, or protect against other things," I said.

"Jimbo said he has his own stone, but what about Dean? We'll need to get him something for protection," Wade said, still grimacing with every movement.

"It says amber is a good choice, it can change negative energy into positive. Now where can we find some amber?" I said, more to myself than expecting Wade to have a solution.

"Send Jimbo a text, he'll probably know where it can be found. He knows way more about the spiritual world than he wants to admit." I fired off a text to him and didn't get a response, but I didn't expect one. He was probably driving here from Coloma.

"I want to bring the ovilus and a spirit box. I'd like to see if we can get any of the spirits there to speak to us."

"They will, they're not even trying to be quiet or stay hidden. They seem to want to be heard, but I'm not sure why. The little girl helped me, but I don't understand why she's here. She should have moved on with the Chalmers," Wade said. "You might get more than you bargained for if we give them a way to openly communicate with us. We can't take any chances, Jason, we'll have to be completely sure of every last detail."

"We will, and we'll make sure Dean is with us. I know he's not comfortable with going down there, but he has to go, or we won't be able to help him." My phone chimed with a text. "Jimbo's on his way, he said he'll stop at Janis's house and get an amber stone for Dean."

"Great, I'm going to find some ibuprofen, and maybe something to eat," Wade said as he struggled to stand, and swayed a little once he was on his feet, before he got his balance.

"You sure you're up to this? We can put it off for a few days." I reached out to help him, but he pushed past me as he walked to the kitchen.

"I'm sure, and we can't wait. The longer we put it off, the harder it's going to be to convince them to leave. And we need to figure out who or what the master is. I still have no clue about that one," he said, his eyes going unfocused as he appeared to be remembering something.

"What is it?" I asked.

"Nothing," he said, and shook his head, which threw him off-balance.

"Babe, be careful." I came up behind him and nuzzled into his neck. "I don't want you hurt any worse than you were." His head dropped forward and he laced his fingers with mine and held our joined hands to his chest.

"I'll be careful, and I won't go off on my own."

I kissed the side of his head, and after eating and double-checking we had everything, Wade talked to Janis. Hopefully he got some good advice while we waited for Jimbo to arrive, and I made sure we had everything packed in the car. He drove up just as Wade was hanging up, and we all set out together for The Hitching Post.

DEAN WAS WAITING RIGHT by the door and let us in as soon as we walked up. "Anxious today?" I asked him.

"I don't like this at all. I really want to get it over with and put this all behind me," he answered.

"Jimbo has a stone for you, they'll give us all a little boost of power and protection. Jimbo? You have the stone for Dean, right?"

"Yeah, I talked to Janis, and she agreed that amber would be best for you," Jimbo explained as he stepped over to Dean. It was the first time he'd been civil to the guy since we'd been helping him.

Wade and I stood by as he explained to Dean that he should put the stone in his right front pocket and keep his thoughts positive. "We'll need to do a cleansing up here before we go down," Jimbo instructed.

"I have everything we need." I took out my go bag and handed Wade and Jimbo some bundles of herbs. Jimbo handed a feather to Dean and showed him how to fan the smoke everywhere in the restaurant.

"You're sure this will help?" Dean asked Jimbo.

"I hope so, these guys know what they're doing, listen to them. They won't let you down, we just need to do what Janis told us," he replied, raising his voice to shout that last bit to Wade and I. We looked at each other and smiled. When we were finished, we all stood around a table that held the equipment we'd use this time.

"Okay, everyone has their stones?" Everyone patted their pockets and nodded. "I want to take the ovilus and a spirit box. Jimbo, are you okay to take the ovilus and an EVP meter?"

"Fuck, if I have to."

"You do." I stared him down, and he slumped and reached for the two devices.

"Wade, you and I will take the spirit box and a recorder. We don't want to miss any clues we might get while we're down there. Everyone take a flashlight and extra batteries, I'm not getting stuck in the dark again. We'll all be staying in the basement, I don't want anyone wandering into the other area. We'll also take some herb bundles and attempt to cleanse the area, but since it's not completely separate from the outer area, I don't see it working."

Everyone nodded, and we started to move to the basement door. I stood with my hand on the knob, then turned to face them. "Everyone be careful. Wade, especially you." He nodded and leaned in to press his lips to mine.

I took a deep breath and opened the door.

CHAPTER FIFTEEN

WADE

I STOOD close to Jason's back as he opened the door to the basement. It looked like it had the first night we'd come; the light was on and illuminated the stairway that led to the dirt floor beneath. Jason reached back and squeezed my leg.

"Stay close," he whispered, and I squeezed his shirt tighter to signal I'd heard him.

We all made our way down, one after the other, and when we entered the basement, nothing seemed out of order. The boards that had separated the basement area were still knocked loose, from where I'd gone through before Jason and Jimbo had rushed through to help me. A shiver wriggled down the length of my body, and I knew I was sensing what I couldn't see.

"Where do you want to use the spirit box?" I asked Jason.

"I think we should go to the farthest corner, while Jimbo and Dean stay near the bottom of the stairs." I nodded and clung to him as we slowly made our way to the corner. The basement wasn't huge, but it was large enough that we'd be challenged to hear Jimbo and Dean. They stood together and took out the ovilus, and Jimbo seemed to be explaining how it worked while Dean looked on.

"They're cute," I said to Jason. He stopped messing with his own gadget to look over at them.

"Yep, but Jimbo's a dick. No one will put up with that shit."

"Maybe he just needs the right person," I said as I watched them. Jason turned to look straight at me before dissolving into laughter. Jimbo and Dean both looked up from their device, confused looks on their faces. "Don't mind him, you know how he gets, Jimbo." I tipped my head in Jason's direction, which made him laugh even harder.

"Not the time, Jason," I said, trying not to move my lips. He fought for control, but it still took him a full minute before he was ready to get down to business.

We stepped closer to our corner, and Jason turned on the ovilus. It immediately crackled to life with the sound of stilted static. I turned to Jason. "What should we ask?"

"Let's see if we pick anything up without asking first." He waved it around the area, and it would go quiet for a moment before blaring back to life.

"Can you make anything out?" I asked.

"No, just static." He walked toward the far corner, the one he'd gone to when we'd first come down here. The ovilus crackled with static then sputtered to silence. It was so quiet I was about to suggest Jason to check the battery, but then I thought I could just make out a word, or really a name.

"Wade?" My name? I would have sworn that's what I heard. Jason turned and met my gaze.

"Waaaadeeee," it said again, this time more clearly, and drawing it out, sounding more like a hiss than someone speaking my name.

"What do you want?" Jason asked.

"Releeeeeeease," it said, once again in the hissing voice that didn't sound quite human. I looked at Jason, and saw my fear reflected back at me.

"Wade," he whispered. "Come here, closer." He held his arm out for me, and I slid right into his side. "Are you okay? Any pain?"

"I'm . . . okay. It said my name," I whispered back.

"I heard it, but stay with me, we'll be fine. Do you feel your stone?" I felt outside my right pocket and could make out the lump of red jasper that was tucked safely inside.

"I have it. You have yours?" I asked, needing to know he was safe too.

"I do, and I have you, we got this, Wade. Don't let the spirits shake you, that's what they're trying to do," he said.

"Are there many here? I can get wisps of their emotions. They're afraid, but not all of them. I can feel one that's angry, it has the strength to rip a hole into our world if it wants. It's waiting for something, but I'm not sure what."

"Are you safe?" he asked. He looked terrified but determined, and I raised my hand to his cheek, hoping to give him a small amount of comfort.

"I am now." The ovilus crackled to life again with another message.

"Nooottt saaaaaaaaaaaaaaffe." Jason pulled me close enough to make my ribs scream in pain. I looked across the basement at Jimbo and Dean, just in time to see Jimbo flung against the brick wall.

"Jimbo," I shouted, as Dean ran right over to him.

The ovilus crackled again. "Diiiiiiiiieeeeeeeeeee."

Jason looked at me, turned it off, and pulled me over to Jimbo. Dean stood frozen a few feet from where Jimbo was crumpled in a heap on the damp ground. My head pounded and my ribs protested, but none of that mattered. Jason released my hand when we were next to Dean and rushed to Jimbo. I started to move that way, but Jason held his hand up.

"Wait right there, I don't want you getting hurt," he said, which annoyed the hell out of me, but my pounding head told me it was the right choice. He carefully knelt in front of Jimbo, from here I could see he was still out cold. I turned to look at Dean; his hand covered his mouth, and his eyes were wide with shock. He still had the spirit box clenched in his other hand, which was fisted at his side.

"Dean? Are you hurt?" I asked. He didn't answer for a second, but slowly he turned to face me, and handed me the spirit box. I took it from him and looked over at Jason.

"Is he hurt, Jason? We should get out of here," I said.

His head snapped up and he glanced at me before leaning in closer to Jimbo. "Jimbo, can you hear me?" He didn't move for a second. Jason moved closer and shook him, trying to get him to react. The moment he touched his arm, the ovilus came to life, startling Jason, who still held it. "It's off, what the fuck is going on?" Jason said.

"James," it said, followed by loud static, then, "die!" It seemed to scream, and Jason jumped at the sudden blast of noise. I tried to move toward Jimbo, but Dean pushed past me and was at his side.

"We need to get the hell out of here," Dean shouted, his eyes still wide. Jason moved to one side of Jimbo, and Dean followed his lead. They put their arms around Jimbo and lifted him from the floor. We all moved quickly toward the door as the lights started to flicker. I noticed movement to my left, and slowly turned my head to look, knowing it wouldn't be anything good.

There was a shimmer in the air, the light outline of

something trying to burst into this world from the veil. With a crackle of electricity, the lights flashed more rapidly, and the little girl appeared. She looked behind her, before meeting my eyes. "Wade, I can't hold him back for long. He will try to kill you all if you stay here much longer." I looked at her, and then at Jason, Jimbo, and Dean. Their backs were to me, they didn't see her, and didn't appear to hear her.

"Wade, you need to go," she shouted, and blinked out of sight. I was stunned for a moment.

Jason turned back to me. "Wade, stay with me, don't get too far behind." I nodded and rushed to his side. As soon as we were on the stairs, the lights stopped flashing and the lower door slammed shut. We all froze at the noise and rushed as fast as we could to the top of the stairs, and practically fell back into the dining area. Jason reached for me and squeezed my hand. Once again, I asked myself, *what the fuck are we doing?*

CHAPTER SIXTEEN

JASON

DEAN and I half carried Jimbo to a small sofa and laid him down, he'd yet to gain consciousness. "Dean, can you get some towels, ice, and a bottle of water?"

"Sure thing," he said, before he jogged off in the direction of the kitchen.

"Wade," I said, stepping over to him and gathering him into my arms.

"I'm okay, why did it hurt Jimbo? So far, none of the spirits have paid any attention to him? What was different this time?" he whispered into my shoulder.

"I'm not sure, have you looked at what messages were left on the spirit box? Maybe that'll give us a clue."

"No, but I did see something before we left the basement. The same little girl appeared again, Jason."

"It doesn't make sense for her to be here, you're sure it's the same girl?"

He looked at me like I'd lost my mind. "I'm sure. She spoke to me again, said she couldn't hold him back much longer, and if we didn't leave soon, he'd kill us."

"What the hell?" I said. Jimbo's groan pulled our attention back to him. "Jimbo? Are you hurt? What happened?" I kneeled down in front of him. I didn't see any obvious injuries, but he'd flown a few feet before hitting that wall, so I wasn't sure he was uninjured.

"Jason, give him a minute," Wade said, resting his hand on my shoulder. He squatted down next to me, and patted Jimbo's cheek. "Jimbo? Can you hear me?" His eyes shot open and he scrambled to back away, causing him to fall off the sofa. He landed with a thud and clambered away from us. "Whoa, dude. You're safe, it's me and Jason." He looked around, his eyes darting all around the room. Dean chose that moment to return with the items I'd asked him for. Jimbo whipped his head around to look at him, and I wasn't sure he recognized him.

"Jimbo. It's okay, I'm not here to hurt you. It's me, Dean, I just went to get you some water and a few things to help clean you up. Is that okay?" Dean explained, hands out in front of him like he was comforting a wild animal, his voice calm.

"I know who you are, asshole. You're the dumbass that brought us here to begin with. You need to tell us what you opened down there. Something's not right. The cleansing should have protected us. What the fuck is going on, Dean?"

"I—I, Jimbo, I didn't do anything. I've only had this place for a few months." He knelt next to Jimbo and slowly took his hand. I looked over at Wade to see him staring at the two of them. "If I had known I would put you in harm's way by calling you, I never would have. I have no idea what's going on, I want this all to end." He whispered that last bit, as he leaned closer to Jimbo.

Jimbo stared at him, disbelief and anger seeming to fight for dominance in his expression. "I barely knew you, Dean.

We went out that one time and I never heard from you again. I thought I said something that pissed you off, which is highly likely." He lifted his hand and rubbed the back of his head and winced.

"You didn't do anything, I was just young and stupid. I had such big dreams, I didn't want to risk any of it by starting a relationship. I was just beginning culinary school, and you were on your way out. It seemed like there was no hope. I thought if we hooked up, I'd get you out of my system, but all it did was make me want you more. I took the job at The Vineyard House just to be closer to you, even when I knew we couldn't start anything. I couldn't stand to not try to be near you," Dean confessed.

Wade and I looked back and forth between the two of them. I couldn't believe what I was hearing. Jimbo was brash, rude, and even though he admitted there had been something briefly between them, it sure as hell sounded like there was much more. Or there could have been.

Wade cleared his throat before he spoke. "Jimbo, are you hurt?" Jimbo didn't move for a second, his gaze locked on where Dean still held his hand. He shook his head, not taking his eyes off their hands. Wade nodded and stepped to where the spirit box had fallen to the floor. He picked it up and turned it on. I stepped closer to his side so we could both see what text would appear.

Wade
Sister
Alone
Hate
Kill
Kill
Kill

"What does it say?" Jimbo asked, grimacing as Dean held ice wrapped in a towel to his head.

"We'll talk about it later," I said as I walked over to my bag and put the spirit box and the ovilus inside. "When we get home, we'll go over it all together." Jimbo squinted his eyes while he watched me, seeming to weigh my words.

"Let's go to Wade's, I need to talk to Deidre," Jimbo said. Dean stopped what he was doing and gave Jimbo a hard look before continuing to hold ice to the back of his head.

"Does he need a doctor?" I asked Dean.

"I'm not sure, he has a small cut and a big bump, but I don't think it's serious," Dean answered.

"I'm okay," Jimbo mumbled, looking embarrassed and pissed at the same time. He took the towel from Dean, and for a second something passed between them, and the way they looked at each other seemed to hold some raw feelings neither of them seemed ready to deal with. He cleared his throat and Dean looked down at the floor. "I'm okay," he said again, this time with a little more insistence.

"Let's get everything cleaned up and go to Wade's, we can listen to any recordings we picked up and look at all of the messages on the spirit box. Dean, did you want to go—"

"No. Jason, we need to go look at what information we gathered. Dean, I'll call you tomorrow. Thanks for helping," Jimbo said, shocking us all. None of us knew how to react to what he'd said, so we all stared at him, waiting for more.

"James, if you don't want me to go, at least be man enough to say it. Don't use the investigation as an excuse. I get it, you're not interested," Dean said, then turned to walk back in the kitchen area. "You guys can see yourselves out, I need to get a few things out of my office. Thanks for coming by so soon." Once again, Wade and I looked between him and Jimbo, finally settling on Jimbo when Dean was out of the room.

"Jimbo, what the fuck just happened?" Wade asked.

"Fuck you, Wade, I'm not saying shit. I want to talk to Deidre." He folded his arms and showed us his familiar scowl.

I breathed out before I said anything, trying to figure out exactly what we should do. "All right, then, let's go to Wade's. You sure it's safe for Dean to be here alone?" At the exact moment I said it, the basement door slammed hard, the sound reverberating through the quiet restaurant.

"Fuck, go ask him to go with us," Jimbo said, and he hung his head and held it in his hands. Wade looked at me in confusion; I'm sure I wore the same expression. This whole situation was weird.

CHAPTER SEVENTEEN

WADE

"I'LL GO TALK TO HIM," I offered, and started to follow Dean.

"Wade, wait here, I don't want you going off by yourself," Jason said, moving closer to me and squeezing my hand. I nodded and stood closer to Jimbo as Jason went after Dean.

"Are you really okay?" I asked him. "You hit that wall pretty hard."

"I'm fine, fuck, you guys are such worriers," he snapped back.

"We care, get the fuck over yourself already."

He leaned away from me and looked at me in shock. "Geez, Wade, I didn't know you had it in you." A smile slowly spread on his lips. "Fuck, I could use a smoke," he grumbled.

"Oh my god, is that why you've been so difficult to be around, I mean more difficult than your normal difficult?"

"Yep, I'm trying to quit, it sucks."

"Good for you, Jimbo, it can't be easy. But maybe try to tone down the attitude a bit. You were really rude to Dean, and he actually was concerned about you. He didn't have to go with us down there, even though we told him he did. He's paying us, he could have broken our contract."

He scrubbed his hand over his head, before wiping it down his face. "I'll talk to him, I just didn't want him to get his hopes up," he said, a bit of sad reluctance in his tone.

"What do you mean?"

Jimbo stood and turned, his back to the direction Dean and Jason had walked, and took a moment to collect his thoughts. "He wasn't lying, when we hooked up, there was a spark. Something I haven't felt many times, and something that we both acknowledged. But I also knew after what happened at The Vineyard House, that I'd be putting him in danger. It almost killed me to push him away then, and we'd barely known each other. The thought of getting to know him more, and having to reject him . . . I just couldn't. I don't want to hurt him, but I don't want him paying for my stupid ability. I won't put him or anyone else in danger."

"You don't get to decide that, James. I make my own decisions," Dean said as he walked right up to Jimbo and got in his face. "It's not up to you." He took Jimbo's face with both hands and kissed him hard. Jimbo stumbled back, but Dean didn't let go, he held on to him until Jimbo regained some control and put his hands on Dean's shoulders. His fingers clawed at Dean's shirt, like he wanted to pull him closer, but also wanted to push him away at the same time.

Dean pulled back and looked Jimbo in the eye. "You're going to tell me everything, and you're going to stop this bullshit that you think you're saving me. I'm done with these games, you've pushed me away long enough." With that he reached behind Jimbo's neck, pulled him in and soundly kissed him again. Jimbo's eyes remained closed after Dean pulled away, and he seemed to need to shake himself out of whatever trance he was in.

"Fine . . . fine. But you're not going to like what you find out. Go with us, you can't stay here alone. No one should be in here alone. What you've got going on downstairs is dangerous for anyone that comes in here," Jimbo said, and surprising us all, he reached out for Dean's hand. Dean took it and jerked on it, probably showing Jimbo he wasn't forgiven.

I looked to Jason, who shrugged and gathered up the few things we'd left out. "Jimbo, do you need to go to the hospital?" Jason asked. Jimbo felt the back of his head and shook it.

"I'm fine, I'll probably need some ice and ibuprofen later, but for now I'm okay."

"Let's get out of here, I need a break from all . . . this," Jason said, waving his hand around Jimbo.

"Whatever, fucker," Jimbo mumbled, as Dean pulled him along toward the door.

After locking up, it was decided Jimbo would ride with Dean to my house. Well, Dean decided, Jimbo seemed to have learned there was no arguing with Dean and had given up on trying. Jason and I walked to the car, and once we were inside with the doors shut, we both turned to look at each other.

"I don't know what's stranger: the fact that a ghost flung Jimbo into a wall, or that Dean called him on his shit and he backed down," Jason said. Our eyes met and we both laughed, which made my head hurt, making Jason pull me close and kiss the side of my head. "Let's get you home." Jason started the car, and I leaned back in my seat.

WE PULLED up to the house, and as soon as I opened the door, Mom was in my face. "Wade, are you okay? Jimbo told me you'd been hurt. Why didn't you call?"

"Because I was fine, Mom, I didn't want to worry you. Jason took care of me." She looked unconvinced and proceeded to poke at me. When she touched my ribs, I flinched and bit my lip to try to control the yelp that threatened.

"You're such a liar, and not a very good one at that. Get your ass in the house and show me what's wrong." She left no room to argue with her, as she stomped off toward my house, leaving me slightly scared to follow her. I turned to look at Jason. His lip pulled up and he snickered at me, I flipped him off over the top of the car.

"Thanks for all the support, babe," I said, and closed the car door.

He held his hands up in surrender. "Hey, I told you to call her."

"Yep, you did." I followed her into the house, and after twenty minutes of her poking at my head and ribs, she finally believed me that I wasn't fatally wounded.

"Where's James?" she asked. Jason and I shared a look before he answered.

"He's on his way, he's bringing a friend."

"Oh, good. That man needs more friends. He works and hangs out with you two, that's his life. He's still young, he needs to find himself someone to go do things with."

"Yes, ma'am," I said. She stopped, turned around, and squinted her eyes at me, before planting her hands on her hips.

Just as my mom was ramping up for another lecture, a car pulled up. She moved to the door to look out, and when she saw it was Jimbo, she walked out to him. "James, it's about time you got here," she scolded. Jimbo got out of the passenger side while Dean stepped out of the driver's side.

"Oh, hello. I'm Wade's mom, Deidre."

"Hello, Deidre, I'm Dean, James's—friend."

She walked over and looped her arm with his, ignoring Jimbo. "Come on, you boys have some explaining to do," she said to Jimbo, who fell in step behind her.

CHAPTER EIGHTEEN

JASON

"JASON, TELL ME WHAT HAPPENED," his mom demanded.

"Mom, I told you I'm fi—"

"Stop right there, young man, I want to hear what happened, not your version. And I know Jason won't lie to me, if he knows what's good for him." She pinned me with a look that reminded me of when we were kids and had done any of a multitude of things that pissed her off.

"He fell into an abandoned mine we didn't know was there," I blurted—damn her and the mom-look.

"Wade! Tell me the whole story." Wade told her everything, how we'd gone down there hoping to just explore a little and ended up with Wade being trapped and hurt. Deidre held her hand over her mouth as she listened, shock and worry evident in her expression.

"You went to the hospital and were checked out?" she asked.

"Yes, I had a slight concussion, bruised my ribs, and needed a cut on my forehead glued," Wade quietly told her.

"Oh, baby, I'm so glad you weren't hurt any worse. You could have been killed."

"I know, Mom, I'm sorry I didn't tell you, I didn't want to worry you," Wade explained.

"I want you to promise me you won't take chances like that again. If Janis tells you to do something that will keep you safe, please do it." He nodded at her and reached for my hand.

"Deidre, I want you to meet someone," Jimbo started, looking more nervous than I had ever seen him. "This is Dean, Dean Peterson. He's . . . important," he said, still looking nervous and unsure.

Deidre stepped closer to Dean, and I wasn't surprised when she enveloped him in a hug. "Very nice to meet you properly, Dean. Sorry you had to see me ripping into my son, but apparently, even though he's a grown-ass man, I still need to remind him to be careful and not go off half-cocked."

"Uh, nice to meet you, Deidre," he said, face muffled into her shoulder and eyes wide with shock.

"So, you're James's new boyfriend?" she asked, as she let Dean loose and gave Jimbo her death stare. It didn't seem to have much effect on him, or he was really good at pretending it didn't.

"He's not my boyfriend, we knew each other years ago. We haven't seen each other since," Jimbo said. Dean looked between Jimbo and Deidre like he wasn't quite sure who to keep his eyes on. "Can we just focus on what happened earlier?" Jimbo asked.

"What happened?" Deidre asked.

"Jimbo was attacked. We all were in the basement, and this time we had done everything Janis told us to do. But for some reason it was still able to attack," I said as I removed the equipment we'd used earlier from my bag.

"James, are you okay? What happened?" Deidre asked. She rushed over to Jimbo and started prodding him, apparently looking for injuries.

"I'm fine, just a bump on the head, that's all." As soon as the words left his mouth, Wade's mom pulled his head forward so she could examine it.

"James, this looks serious, I can take you to the hospital right now. I can't stand that two of my babies are hurt."

Wade's mom continued to examine his head, and Jimbo pulled away from her. "Your 'babies'? What are you talking about, Deidre?"

"Stop it, James, you know you're my baby too."

"Oh god, can we look at the information we got while we were in the basement?" Wade asked. Deidre pulled back her hand to pop him in the head, but hesitated, and kissed his temple instead.

"Please be careful, Wade, I can't take any of you being in danger."

"I know, Mom, we tried to be careful the second time, I'm not sure what happened."

"I know what happened," I said. "The spirits that are in the basement are trapped there, but I'm not sure why, or how. They're angry, and they want to leave but can't. Let's see if there are any clues on the spirit box."

I turned it on and scrolled through the messages, before I came to one that made the blood run from my face and a chill run through me.

I've waited long enough.

"What does it mean?" Wade asked from over my shoulder.

"I'm not sure. I think we may need to talk to your friend

in the basement. She seems to know more about this than we do," I said.

"And how do you think we'll go about that?" Wade asked.

"Jimbo, we're gonna need you to use your ability to pull in some spirits while we're in the basement," I said, Wade looked at me in shock, while Jimbo scowled at me.

"I won't let James be hurt again," Dean said, voice full of conviction. Jimbo looked at him and struggled not to react to his words.

Deidre, on the other hand, did not hold back. "Fuck that, none of you are going back down there until we talk to Janis," she snapped.

We all flinched at her words, but it was Jimbo who spoke up. "You're right, it's time to bring in the cavalry before things get any more out of control. I'll call my sister. This should be good," he grumbled as he took out his phone.

CHAPTER NINETEEN

WADE

I WATCHED as Jimbo dialed the number for Janis and listened in as he talked to her. He nodded along for a few seconds, before locking eyes with Jason. None of this could be good.

He ended the call, and Dean walked over to him and gave him a hard look. "What is it, James? What did she say?"

"She said there's a spirit trapped down there. It's been there a long time and it doesn't want to leave. It's keeping the other spirits trapped with it, to siphon off their power. It won't go away without a fight. It's going to try to take us all out so it can continue to exist. All it cares about is surviving."

"So, what do we do?" I asked. Jason and Jimbo knew way more about this shit than I did.

"We're going to have to spend more time there, like we did at The Vineyard House. We'll try to contact the spirits and see if they'll give us any clues, so far they've been very cryptic. The only spirit we've actually seen is the little girl Wade interacted with," Jason said.

"What little girl?" Jimbo asked.

"The same one we saw at The Vineyard House, she was at the top of the stairs, just for a short time before she disappeared again," I answered.

"When is a good time for us to stay the night, Dean?" Jason asked.

"I'm not sure that's a good idea. Don't get me wrong, I want the ghost, or spirits, or whatever they are, gone. But I won't have James or anyone else hurt."

"Wait, I thought Janis said not to be there after dark, that it was too dangerous," Deidre said.

"She did, but something has changed. She said if we don't convince the main spirit to cross over soon, we may not ever be able to. It knows what we want to do and doesn't want to leave. It has some attachment to the area that she couldn't explain. Only that it doesn't want to leave," Jimbo explained.

"I'm so sorry I got all of you involved in this," Dean said as he let his head drop into his hands. "I thought it was just a simple haunting—you'd come in, burn some sage, and send the spirit packing. I had no idea it would be this complicated."

"At least you recognized what was causing the problem and acknowledged it, most people don't," I said. "It took staying at a real haunted house to really make me believe it all. Jason dragged me to so many places that were supposed to be haunted, and nothing happened. Which, I'm not gonna lie, I was fine with. But he wanted to see something so bad, and I had such a big crush on him, I'd have gone anywhere to spend some time with him." Jason grasped my hand and squeezed it, and Mom released a dreamy sigh, making us both laugh.

"Dean, there's a lot I need to tell you. I know you don't

understand why we never got together again, and I know I need to explain, but right now, we need to work on getting those spirits out of your restaurant. Janis said the longer we leave them, the stronger they'll get. The one holding them there is very old, and he's been keeping other sprits trapped for years. I want to help, but I don't want to put you in danger," Jimbo said.

"I—" Dean started, before Jimbo cut him off.

"I know you want to help, and you can. But we'll need to be careful. I have an ability that connects me with the other side of the veil. I'm able to control it, but it takes everything in me to do it. If I don't completely control my emotions, I can't control my power," Jimbo explained, surprising us all with his willingness to open up.

"James? What are you saying?" Dean asked. My mom wore a sad expression, as we waited for Jimbo to say the words that could change how Dean felt about him.

"I'm what you would call a beacon, spirits are drawn to me. They always have been. Through the years, my sister has helped me learn how to dampen my light, so they can't find me as easily. But they still do. I can control it if I keep my emotions under control, but if I'm stressed, or worried, it makes it much harder to keep myself hidden from them. When you're with us in that basement, I can't keep myself under control. I'm too worried what danger I could be putting you in."

"I can take care of myself. I did everything you told me to do. You guys did the sage thing, I thought that would protect me?" Dean asked.

"It will, but it won't hold back what I could invite if I can't control the beacon. My emotions are my weakness, and they'll put you at risk if you're anywhere near me when the spirits decide to try to make contact." Dean stood up and knelt in front of Jimbo, resting his hand on his knee.

"James, I'm in this with you. If you want me there, I'm there, but if you think it'll put everyone in danger, I'll stay away. I just want to keep you safe," Dean said.

Jimbo's eyes never left Dean's while he spoke. When he finished, Jimbo reached out and cupped his cheek. "What if I want you there? What if I've always wanted you there?" Jimbo whispered to him, before Dean covered his hand with his own. The look that passed between them spoke of years of yearning, and a lot of hurt.

"What if I want to be there—be with you, more than I've ever wanted anything?"

"What the hell just happened?" Jason whispered to me. My mom leaned over and slapped him, breaking the spell that seemed to have fallen over all of us.

Jimbo blinked his eyes and slowly tore his gaze away from Dean. "You fuckers," he mumbled, right before Dean took his face in his hands and kissed him again, as my mom squealed in that deafening pitch that, sadly, I was getting used to hearing.

CHAPTER TWENTY

JASON

"JIMBO, can you give us a little more detail? I mean, I'm sorry to interrupt your . . . lovefest and all, but if we want to clear the spirits out of Dean's restaurant, we need to know everything. No more holding back."

He met my eyes for a moment before he breathed out a long breath. "I told you about being a beacon, but I left out how powerful the draw is, and how hard it is to control. If I open it up, every spirit within miles will be drawn to me. And they won't be happy about it, they're drawn like steel to a magnet, and when they get there, they're pissed. I can control it, but it's connected to my emotions, so being in a constant state of anger, or frustration, keeps it locked down. But if I'm happy, or feeling love, they're drawn in a way I can't control."

"What if we make a ghost trap? We can draw them in, trap them, and then send them on their merry way," I said. When no one said anything, I explained, "There's a few ways to do it, hallowed ground in a metal box, or a candle in a jar. We could also trap them in a crystal."

"Have you actually tried any of these?" Wade asked.

"You know I haven't, but I'm pretty sure they could work."

"The spirit in the basement is like nothing I've felt before, not that I've opened myself up to many spirits," Jimbo said.

"When do you want to go back? We should do it soon," I said. We all looked at Dean, waiting for his answer, and dreading it at the same time.

"How is Sunday night? I can close early so we have time to set up before dark."

"What do you mean 'we'? I think it's better if you're not there, Dean," Jimbo said, still holding on to Dean's hand.

"Jimbo, I think we should try to set up our equipment similar to the way we did at The Vineyard House. We'll put a laser grid in that lower area by the mineshaft, we can set up cameras in the basement, and use the ovilus to see if anyone is willing to talk. I'm betting if you're right, and they're being trapped by one main spirit, they'll be willing to try to help us to help them, if given the chance."

"Jason, they want to leave, it's kept some of them there when all they want is to be with their family. I don't understand why, but the little girl spirit that talked to me seemed concerned for it. Maybe we should see if she'd be willing to talk to us a little more," Wade said.

Clapping my hands together, I stood. "Okay then, let's spend the next couple of days getting ready for Sunday. Wade, you and I need to map out where we'll put the equipment and what each of us will be doing when we're there. Everyone bring your stones. I'm not sure why we need them, but I trust Janis."

"They didn't keep Jimbo safe. He had his in his pocket,

and I had mine, but he was thrown into a wall. We're damn lucky he wasn't seriously injured," Dean said.

"You're right, but we can't take the chance. We should do everything we can to protect one another," Wade said. "Let's all get some sleep, and we'll talk more tomorrow."

"Are you okay, baby?" I asked. He looked so tired, his eyelids seemed to droop more and dark circles were visible under his eyes. He melted into the couch like he was ready to pass out.

"Yeah, just tired, and a little sore."

"Wade, I want you to get some sleep, go on now. Jimbo, Dean, sorry to kick you out, but you can see Wade needs to get some sleep," Deidre said. "James, will you be all right to drive home?"

"Yeah, I'm fine, just rattled me a bit."

"It did more than rattle you, you're lucky you didn't need stitches," Dean added.

Finally everyone was gone, and it was just Wade and I. I put my hand out to help him stand, and he swayed a little on his feet. "Are you sure you're okay?"

He leaned in closer to me, and I put my arm around his back. "Yeah, just want to go to bed."

"Your wish is my command." I nearly had to carry him there, he was falling asleep on his feet; this day had taken more out of him than he was willing to admit. I worried his injury was worse than we realized, as I helped him sit on the bed. He slumped back on the pillows without his eyes ever opening. As I eased his shirt over his head, and slid his shorts off, he still hadn't moved. He rolled to the side and was asleep before I could undress and lay down next to him. I settled in next to him, and was just about to close my eyes when he reached his hand across the sheet, searching me out. I smiled before clasping his hand in mine and leaning in to kiss his lips lightly. "I love you, Wade Rivers, I always have," I whispered.

THE DREAM BEGAN like most did—I was outside with Wade, we were lying in the grass, counting stars in my backyard and having a quiet conversation. And as happens in dreams, we were suddenly in the basement of Dean's restaurant. Wade was over in the far corner with his back to me. He was facing the wall, and almost seemed to be in a conversation with someone. I stood and watched him for a few moments, before moving in his direction. When he became aware of me, he turned with a smile and reached out his hand.

"Jason, come here, I want you to meet someone," he said, wearing a big smile I couldn't help but return. "This is Emma." He moved to the side to reveal a little girl, the same little girl we'd seen at The Vineyard House. "Go ahead, Emma, tell Jason what you told me."

She bowed her head for a moment, seeming unsure, before looking up at us both. "Hello, Jason, I'm very pleased to meet you," she said with a slight bow. "I've been trying to help Wade, but he needs more help than I can give him."

"What do you mean?" I asked. When I glanced at Wade, he looked frozen in place. He didn't move at all and wore a blank expression as he stared off with unseeing eyes. "Wade?"

"He's okay, I need you to listen to me. You understand the way of the veil better than Wade does, he was easier for me to make contact with, but he'll need your help. There is a force in the basement that must be controlled, or soon it will grow too strong and there will be no stopping it."

"Did you help him when he fell into the mineshaft?" I asked.

"Yes, he was injured, and I couldn't stop that from happening, but I tried my best to keep the spirits busy so he could escape before something much worse happened to him."

"You realize he could have died, he fell headfirst down into that old mine. Did you have anything to do with that?"

She didn't answer, just looked over to Wade and back to me. "Unless you force this spirit to move on, something worse will happen. It will keep attacking you, and every time you come back, it'll be stronger. You will need all of your powers combined to accomplish this, or eventually it will kill one of you, then that spirit will be added to the fray," she said.

"What do you mean?"

"If you die in this basement, your spirit will never leave. You will be trapped in the fray forever, and you'll be part of the force that resides there."

"Fuck this, I won't put anyone at risk to chase away a spirit that's willing to kill us to stay. I won't put my friends in danger, and no way I'll let Wade near it," I snapped at her.

She smiled at me, as though I hadn't yelled at her at all. "Jason, you'll do what you need to do. It can be done, but it won't be easy." She turned and drifted back to where she'd been when I first walked over, standing in front of Wade. He seemed to snap to life, and smiled at me like nothing strange had happened.

I startled awake, my gaze immediately meeting Wade's own. "Are you okay?" he asked.

I reached for him and carefully pulled him to me. "I'm

fine, just a weird dream." I stroked his back while he laid his head on my chest.

"Me too, I dreamed I was talking to the little girl I told you I'd seen earlier—"

"You introduced me to her," I finished for him.

He lifted his head off my chest and met my eyes. "What the fu—"

CHAPTER TWENTY-ONE

WADE

"HOW COULD we have the same dream?" Jason asked. He sat up in bed and leaned back against the headboard.

"I'm not sure, you're the expert on all the weird shit. Is that even possible?" He paused for a second, so I continued. "At this point, I think anything's possible. Remember, Janis said I was an empath, and you're aware of spirits, maybe now that we're together, we're linked somehow," I said, trying to think of some explanation. "Janis said we're stronger together, so maybe that has something to do with it."

"I was so worried about you being injured, I couldn't stop thinking of it when I fell asleep. I was so thankful you hadn't been hurt when we returned to the restaurant. Maybe those emotions had something to do with it too," Jason said.

"I have no idea, but if it means we're closer than we were, I can't imagine. You're everything to me, I can't imagine feeling more for you than I already do," I said.

Jason reached his hand out and pulled me into his side.

"Am I hurting you?" he asked, and I felt his lips brush my hair.

"Not at all."

He nuzzled his nose into my hair, making me shiver. "You're sure you're not in pain?" he breathed out.

"No," I whispered, "not even a little."

He rolled me gently onto my back and lightly feathered his lips against mine, igniting a want in me that still burned brighter and brighter each time we were together. "The more I have you, the more I want you, I don't think I'll ever get enough of you," he whispered between soft kisses that made me want more.

"Jason, fuck me." I froze for a second, which made him pull back to meet my eyes.

"What is it? Am I hurting you?"

"No, I just realized, a few months ago I would never have dreamed I'd be saying that to you. Or that you'd be kissing me and sleeping in my bed. I was afraid to hope, but I'm so glad it came true." I told him this often, but he never made me feel uncomfortable for it, he seemed to sense my need to confirm it was real.

"It's real, baby, it's all real. There's nothing else in this world I want more than you." And then he was kissing me, and I needed to take a breath, but I wanted him to kiss me more.

Finally, I moved my mouth to the side and took a deep, panting breath. He reached over his shoulder and pulled his shirt off, and I ran my fingers over his toned chest, enjoying the smooth feel, and scratching my nails in the few hairs he had. Our eyes locked briefly before he leaned back down and kissed me again, his lips sliding over mine, and his tongue wasted no time in teasing my own in what was now becoming a familiar and enticing way.

He rolled me to my uninjured side, and after making sure—way too many times—that I wasn't in any pain, he was finally pushing slowly into me, and I groaned and arched my back. My ribs complained, but there were so many good sensations, I ignored the pain—but he felt me flinch. He didn't say anything, just trailed his fingertips along my side, nearly tickling me, but as he slowly pressed deeper into me, all I felt was him. My head tipped back on his shoulder, and I felt his warm breath in my ear.

"I love you, Wade, I love you so much," he repeated over and over, gripping my hip and rocking into me as he trailed kisses up my neck and along my jaw. He reached past my hip to my bent knee and pulled it closer to my chest. "Is this okay?" he asked.

"Oh god, yes, harder. I want to feel you tomorrow."

He groaned and started to thrust harder, causing us both to gasp. I reached the arm that I was lying on back and gripped his hair. I didn't have to see him to know his eyes would be rolling back in his head. He had me so on edge already, if he touched me, it would all be over, far too soon.

"I want to come so bad, but I don't want it to end," I groaned. He didn't say a word, just reached for my dick and started stroking. There was nothing but him, he was every touch, every sensation, everything that I'd ever need. "I love you," I managed before my orgasm ripped through me, triggering his. He continued to rock into me as jolts of passion and love rolled through me. Avoiding my ribs as much as he could, Jason pulled me back against his chest, and I could have fallen asleep in his arms with him still inside me.

He kissed my shoulder before moving to pull out of me. We were sweaty, and I knew I'd be sleeping in a wet spot I'd created, but I reached back and held him to me. "Not yet," I said, and held his hand over my heart.

I AWOKE to Jason still wrapped around me, his breath soft on my cheek, and dying of heat. I tried to slip away from his grasp, but he tightened his arms around me. My ribs protested, making me flinch. He was awake in an instant.

"Wade? Are you okay?"

I gritted my teeth to hold back a groan. "Yeah, I'm fine, just stiff from sleeping."

He slid off the bed and was in front of me in an instant with his hand offered. "Come on, let's get you in the shower and see if that helps."

The shower did help, and the ibuprofen helped even more, and afterward we sat at my kitchen table, mapping out the areas of the restaurant we thought would be best for each device.

"We need four cameras in the basement, one on each corner," Jason said. He was in his element, using all the gadgets he'd collected over the years, and trying to prove anything we caught was real. "What do you think of the laser grid down there, too? Maybe we'll get lucky and actually catch some of the activity we know goes on down there."

"That's a good idea, I know we caught some audio interactions on the ovilus and the spirit box, but I'd like to see something visual too," I said as I leaned closer to look at his sketch. "Should we put some motion detectors in the restaurant? I'd feel better knowing we'd be aware if there was something upstairs while we're down there."

He leaned closer into my side and kissed above my ear. "I like how you think," he said, and sketched out the restaurant, highlighting the areas that were most vulnerable, and offered the best views of the whole area.

"Yoo-hoo," Mom called, poking her head in the door. "Are you boys busy?"

"Hey, Mom, come in. We're just planning out our next move. What's going on?"

"I don't want to interrupt you, but I wanted to show you something." She stepped over to where we sat, carrying a box, then setting it down in front of us and opening it up.

"Is that—?" Jason asked.

"Yes! Boys, your shirts and stuff are here." We both jumped up and rummaged through the box, taking out shirts at the same time. A cartoon chicken ran across the front, with the words "Running Scared Paranormal Research" across the back. "Well, what do you think? Too much?" She grabbed the shirt I held and started looking at it closer.

I grabbed it back. "These are awesome! I love them." I said, pulling her in for a hug.

"Looks like we've got our uniforms, now we're ready to get down to business," Jason said, and slipped his shirt over his head. "Now we just need some ghosts." His phone rang right then, and he smiled when he said it, but we both knew he wasn't joking.

CHAPTER TWENTY-TWO

JASON

I HOPED we were all ready for this, but something niggled at the back of my brain, telling me this wouldn't be easy, or safe. I tried to convince Dean he should stay away from the restaurant when we were there, but he refused to listen.

"I'm going, I won't have you, Wade, or James risking your lives for my business," he'd argued.

"Fine, but you make sure you're never alone when we're there. You're glued to Jimbo's side the whole night. Can you promise me that?" I demanded.

"Yes, whatever it takes, but I will be there."

"Fair enough," I said, then hung up. I turned to Wade. "I need to call Jimbo." Wade was still busy with Deidre, looking through the box of shirts and other items she'd ordered for the business. He nodded without pulling his eyes away from the box of business cards he held in his hand.

"Jimbo, I just talked to Dean—" I started, and he promptly cut me off.

"Don't start, Jason, I know he wants to be at the restaurant when we're there, but I've told him it's too dangerous. If he's there, I have no hope of hiding myself from the spirits, and believe me, they will find us."

I listened to him, and realized I was smiling. I must have not responded when he expected me to, because now he was uncharacteristically quiet. "Jimbo? Sorry, I'm listening."

"I'm not kidding here, you'll all be in danger if he's there," Jimbo said, sounding genuinely worried.

"We'll make sure we do everything we can to protect each other. I told him none of us should be alone while we're there. If we look out for each other, we should be fine."

"I don't want to put him . . . or you guys, in danger, I need you to take this seriously," he pleaded.

"I do, I do take all of this seriously. But I really think we're all better off together. And if Dean is there, you two can handle one area, while Wade and I investigate another. We can cover more of the place all at once, and make sure everyone is safe and accounted for."

"Jason, are you sure Wade's up for this? He was hurt pretty bad, I—" I moved into the bedroom, not wanting Wade to overhear us.

"He'll be fine, he won't admit it, but I know he's been in pain. I worry about him going with us, but at least if he's with me the whole time, I know I can keep him safe."

"But you don't know. And I like having Dean around, I'd like to keep it that way if you don't mind," he snapped, sounding more like himself.

"We'll do our best, Jimbo, I promise."

"Make sure you do, I'll see you Sunday." Without another word, he hung up, just as Wade walked into the room.

"Everything okay?" he asked. I reached for him and pulled him into my arms. He flinched when I pressed against his ribs.

"Sorry, still a little tender," he said, and rested his forehead against the side of my head.

"I'll be more careful, I didn't mean to hurt you."

"I know, and your concern makes me love you even more," he said with a laugh. "It sounds so hokey but it's true."

"I don't think it's hokey at all. I'm glad you finally made me realize what I was missing." I held myself back from squeezing him tighter to me, it never seemed to be close enough.

"I'm hungry, what do you think about getting something to eat?"

"I think that sounds like a great idea."

IT SEEMED like time rushed by, and before I could think about it, it was Saturday night. Tomorrow we'd be staying the night at The Hitching Post.

Wade was already in bed when I slipped in next to him. "Don't worry, Jason, we got this. We're all packed and ready to go, and we have everything mapped out for where we'll put the cameras and other equipment. We can't do anything else until we're there."

"You're right, let's get some sleep," I said, and turned off the light. Wade lay his head on my chest, and within moments I was asleep. The soft sound of Wade's breathing was soothing and a constant—then something changed. First, I felt the temperature drop in the room. It was midsummer and hot as hell, and we had the air conditioner on, but it suddenly felt like it was midwinter. I imagined it was cold enough I could see my breath. I curled closer to Wade, hoping to steal some of his warmth, and pulled the blanket up tighter.

The room went deathly quiet then, like a night silenced in a thick blanket of fog. I couldn't hear anything—no cars on the street, no crickets chirping, and not Wade's rhythmic breathing. I breathed in, and it sounded deafening in the total silence of the room. I started to inhale, and became aware of something in the room, something that wasn't there a moment ago, and something that shouldn't be there. I tried to move, to wake Wade and warn him, but I couldn't. My arms and legs were like lead, and my eyes remained closed. My body seemed to anticipate something, but I had no idea what it was, only a sense that I should be afraid.

I felt a weight settle onto the bed next to me, and I hoped it was Deidre, coming in to wake us because we'd slept late, but somehow, I knew it wasn't. I felt the weight lean closer to me, and still I couldn't move. My breathing changed to short pants as I started to panic; I couldn't move, and whatever was sitting on the bed next to me could do whatever it wanted, and there wasn't a damn thing I could do to stop it.

Suddenly a thought hit me: I knew what this was. And in that moment, I knew we had to succeed, or we'd never be free of the influence of whatever was in that basement. In that moment, I knew what was sitting on the bed next to me was one and the same.

As cold fear licked up my spine, I knew without a doubt what we were facing, and what had found us here.

Evil.

I snapped awake and sat up, breathing hard from the

fear that coursed through me, I looked over at Wade and he still slept soundly, unaware that anything was wrong. He'd know soon enough, we all would. The rest of the night was spent wide awake, and going over every detail. Whatever was in that basement had to go, or nothing would be the same ever again.

CHAPTER TWENTY-THREE

WADE

SOMETHING WAS BOTHERING JASON. I could see it in the way his shoulders tensed, and how his eyes darted all around the house, checking and rechecking the equipment we'd packed to take to The Hitching Post.

"Is everything okay? We've done about all we can to be ready," I said, trying to reassure him.

"Yeah, yeah, everything's fine. I just have a feeling this is way more than we're expecting, and it's not going to go as planned. Not that we can plan for how a spirit will react, but I don't think Janis had any idea what's down there, and her protections aren't going to do shit."

I set down the case I was holding and stepped closer to him, putting my hand on his arm. "Is there something you know that you're not telling me?"

He covered my hand with his, closed his eyes, and let his head dip forward. "I'm not sure, I just have a weird feeling about this one."

"You do realize, all of our jobs are weird. We're in the business of clearing out spirits that have become a nuisance. Like I said, weird." I tried to lighten his mood, hoping if he thought I wasn't worried, he wouldn't be either. But deep inside I knew he wouldn't believe me, and he'd still be apprehensive.

"Wade, I know I've said this before, but I need to know you'll do what I say. Do not leave my side when we're in there. Not to check equipment, not to grab a pair of pliers, not even to go to the bathroom. We stick together like glue, you got me?" He gave me a hard look, not of impatience, but more of worry. I held his gaze for a moment before I answered.

"Whatever you say, Jason. I trust you more than anyone. I know you wouldn't put me, or any of us, in danger if you could help it. I'll follow your lead and do whatever you say." His eyes bounced between mine, and whatever he was looking for there, he must have found. He leaned in, and after pressing our foreheads together, he kissed me.

"I love you. Don't ever doubt that," he whispered against my lips.

"I never thought I'd hear you say that, and now that I have, I know it's true. I won't ever doubt you." I meant every word, and I knew by the intensity of his gaze, he did too.

AFTER PROMISING Mom we'd call her if anything happened, we left for the restaurant, hopefully with enough time to spare since it was Sunday evening and traffic was heavier with all the people returning home from their weekend getaways.

When we finally found a parking space a street over from the restaurant, we were half an hour late. I took out my phone and tapped out a quick text to Jimbo, asking where he was. My phone rang almost immediately after I hit Send.

"What the fuck? You guys were supposed to be here a while ago."

"Yeah, sorry. We didn't allow for traffic. Can you help us carry the equipment in?" I asked Jimbo.

"I'll meet you there, don't move," he barked out.

"We'll be here." I slipped my phone into my pocket and turned to look at Jason.

"What did he say?" he asked.

"Same shit, different day," I said with a laugh, and opened the door. Jason met me at the back of the car, and we started gathering everything we'd need, including ten pounds of salt we'd taken from the garage. We didn't get much ice around here, but my dad always worried we would and kept it stocked.

Jimbo sauntered up to the two of us, and without saying a word, started unloading the rest of the equipment. "Hey, man, sorry we were late," Jason said.

"It's okay, traffic was bad for me too, but I left Coloma early. I didn't want to take a chance on it."

"Good thinking. Is Dean inside?" I asked.

"Yes, he's just closing out the last customers, maybe we should wait until everyone leaves. I don't think he'd appreciate us scaring off his clientele." Jimbo took out his phone and tapped on it for a second, then smiled, before he looked at us and realized we were watching him. "Fuckers, don't even say it," he warned.

I walked over to him and clapped my hand on his shoulder. "Jimbo, it's great to see you happy. We haven't known you very long, but this is the happiest I've ever seen you. Good for you."

His eyes widened before he ducked his head. "Yeah, well, he makes me happy."

Jason glanced over at us and tried hide a smile of his

own. "Everyone ready?" he asked, effectively ending the conversation about Jimbo's love life.

"Yep," Jimbo piped in, looking a little too happy to end the conversation.

We walked the short distance to the restaurant, all of us lugging various backpacks and equipment cases. As we approached the door, a couple was just about to leave the restaurant. Dean held the door for them with a smile, as they walked out onto the street. He looked directly at Jimbo and that smile grew, the same way Jimbo had smiled at his phone earlier. Oh my god, these two had it bad.

"Hello, everyone, your timing is perfect, my last customer just left. I let the kitchen staff leave just a few minutes ago. We should be good to go," Dean said.

I started through the door and glanced back at Jason—gone was his usual look of curiosity and adventure, and in its place was an expression I'd never seen on his face at any of the other places we'd visited: fear and dread.

I continued into the restaurant and set down the equipment I'd carried in, and as I stooped down to set it on the floor, I was shoved hard. I turned to look, but no one was near me. When I met Jason's eyes, I could see it again: fear.

CHAPTER TWENTY-FOUR

JASON

I RUSHED OVER to Wade's side as soon as I realized what had happened. "Wade? Are you okay?"

"Yeah, just . . . I got shoved. I didn't see anything, or hear anything, just felt a good hard shove."

He looked around the restaurant, appearing confused at what had just happened. We'd had much worse than that, but not as soon as we'd walked in the door. Something really didn't want us here, and it was making sure we knew it.

I patted him on the back, when I wanted to hug him. "We'll get everything settled in this area and then seal it with the salt, at least nothing else will be able to get in."

"Or get out," he added. I wasn't sure yet if that was good or bad.

Wade did as I asked and stayed close to me. I wasn't sure why it was so important to me, but it was, and I couldn't control the panic that threated to rise up in my chest when I thought about him being out of my sight. "We sketched out how we want everything set up." I spread the paper out on a table for everyone to see. "Jimbo, you and Dean go salt the kitchen and office areas. Wade, you and I will set up the cameras and perimeter alarms in the dining room. Once we're done, we'll draw a hex sign at the door and seal it with salt. We'll know if anything comes in or out while we're in the basement," I explained.

"Are we all going downstairs?" Jimbo asked, with a quick glance at Dean.

"I think you two should stay up here, if anything happens, we can call for help on the walkies. I brought them just in case, I know the phone signal is a little funky down there. Wade and I will go to the basement together, and hopefully we'll be able to convince whatever's down there to leave."

"What if we can't?" Wade asked.

I stepped closer to him and put my arm around him. "We can, and we will. We just need to find out what it wants, and what will make it leave here forever." I tried to show Wade I wasn't afraid, but he knew me too well. I noticed how many times he looked at me with concern, but I tried to let it go. We'd know soon enough what we were up against.

Wade opened the case that held the perimeter alarms and got busy setting them up at the front entrance and the door that led to the basement. I watched him for a moment before taking four cameras and setting them up in various places around the room, so every angle was covered.

"Dean, where should we set up our laptops?" I asked.

"Wherever works for you," he answered.

"Let's put it all in the office, it's a big enough area. We can set up two laptops, and Dean and Jimbo can monitor them while we're down in the basement. They can warn us if they see something we don't," I explained, while they all looked at me.

"Jason, promise me you won't take any crazy chances.

Don't try to be the hero," Jimbo said, as Dean looked at him with a warm look.

"Don't worry, I'm not taking any chances. I won't put any of us in danger. Now, let Wade and I set up the laptops and get the camera feeds up so you can get comfortable with the program." Wade and I made sure everything was up and running, and all views were clear. We tested the perimeter alarm and it worked exactly like it was supposed to.

"Okay, everyone, I'm going to draw some protection signs at the entrance and at the office door, I'll also draw it in front of the basement door. Dean, do you have a problem with that? I have chalk and was going to draw it out on the floor," I explained.

"Jason, do whatever you need to do. I appreciate you trying to be respectful but, honestly, I just want all this behind us," Dean answered, and as he did, Jimbo moved to his side.

"Do it, Jason. I know Janis thought those stones would protect us, but they didn't do shit. I've seen your methods keep us safe, well, as safe as you can be when a lunatic ghost is hell-bent on attacking. I'll help Dean clean up anything he wants me to when we're all done," Jimbo said, and Dean slowly reached his hand out and squeezed Jimbo's.

I nodded and took out the stick of chalk I'd brought and drew the same design I'd used at The Vineyard House. I knew Dean would question it, but I'd leave that for Jimbo. After drawing it, I spread lines of salt at the entrance, and also at the door to the basement.

Next, Wade and I gathered cameras, the laser grid, and another perimeter alarm, and tucked them into a backpack. It also held salt, a couple of recorders, flashlights, and extra batteries. We both wore headlights; I didn't want to take the chance of not having enough light this time. We'd both carry flashlights on us, in addition to the headlights.

"I think we have everything, anything we've missed?" I asked Wade.

"Not that I can think of, I think we're good to go," he said, with a tight smile. Jimbo didn't say anything, but he looked worried.

"Jimbo, can you stay in control of whatever it is that draws ghosts to you? I know we haven't talked about it in detail, but I need to know you can keep it under wraps while we're down there. Can you do that?" I asked.

He took a moment to think about it and rubbed his hand across his shaved head. This time it was him who reached out and took Dean's hand, pulling it close to his chest as he made eye contact with me.

"Jason, I won't put any of you in danger. I'll do my damnedest to keep myself in control. I'm not gonna lie, it's harder to control when I'm emotional, so I'm going to try like hell to not let that happen. I've brought my stone, and I've done everything I can to prepare, but if it feels like I can't control it I'll warn everyone. Because you won't want to be down there if that happens."

He looked at me with such a serious look, it actually scared me. He wasn't joking, and he wasn't exaggerating. He was being completely honest. And knowing that did nothing to ease my fears.

CHAPTER TWENTY-FIVE

WADE

AFTER JASON SEALED the entrances with salt and a hex sign, the air felt a little lighter. Whatever had been there when we'd first arrived seemed to have retreated, or just moved down to the basement. Hopefully the barriers held and kept Jimbo and Dean safe. At least they'd be up here, and not down there. Something scared Jason, I wasn't sure what it was, but he was keeping it from me, and that wasn't like him at all.

"Wade, you ready to go?" he asked, standing just at the door to the basement stairs, backpack slung over his shoulder, and holding another bag that held salt and chalk.

"We're going to salt down there too?" I asked.

"Yes, fuck 'em, we're going to do all we can to take away any power from them."

"I think there's one main one," I said, not really realizing what I'd said.

Jason stopped in his tracks and turned to me. "What makes you say that?"

"I'm not sure, but I think the dream we had told us more than we realized at the time."

He squinted his eyes and seemed to be deep in thought. "It can't be just one, can it? I know you said they're trapped here, why would they be? We don't really know any more than we did before," Jason said, and moved closer to me.

"We do, and we know we're both strong, and stronger together. We got this." He held his hand out for me, and I hefted the backpack higher on my shoulder and took it. I turned the knob and looked over at Jimbo and Dean, they were both standing in front of the office, watching us. Dean looked worried, but Jimbo looked terrified. He had seen what could be down there, and he was probably relived to not have to face it again.

"Turn your walkie on, I want to know we can contact you," Jimbo said, waving his walkie at us. I turned Jason around and reached into his backpack to get it. Turning it on, it came immediately to life with a crackle of static. I clicked the button a couple of times, and Jimbo's walkie reacted.

"Sounds good, let's do this before it gets any later," Jason said. It was already around nine, and since it was summer it was still not completely dark out, but the sun had set, and we didn't have much time left before night was completely upon us.

"Let's go," I said, and continued down the stairs to the bottom. We both stood there for a moment before I reached for the doorknob. The door seemed to pulse with energy, I hoped I was imagining it, but I wasn't willing to bet on it. I turned the knob and the door swung open. The light was on, so the room was illuminated. From where we stood, it all looked as it had the last time we were here, nothing had changed.

"Wade, remember what I said earlier—"

"Stay close," I finished for him. "Don't worry, I'm not

planning on wandering away again anytime soon." He nodded and walked over to one of the crates that were stacked against the wall next to the door. Jason set his backpack down and took out the laser grid, then looked at me and waited for me to walk over to the far side of the building with him. After making sure we had it positioned in a good area, we turned it on and returned to the crates.

"Laser grid is in position," I said into the walkie.

"Guys, be careful," Jimbo said, not even bothering to try to hide his fear.

"We will, we're about to set up the cameras. I'll let you know when we're done, and you can check the feed."

"Roger," he said, completely serious. I met Jason's eyes and we both grinned at each other—and then the lights went out.

"Fuck," I said, and scrambled to turn on the headlight that, luckily, we'd slipped on while we were still upstairs. My fingers grappled with the button to turn it on, and I realized my hands were shaking. The light flooded my immediate area and I blinked, trying to make my eyes focus faster —Jason, where the fuck was Jason? My head whipped around, and the light with it. It was bright, but only a fairly small area was illuminated.

"Jason? Jason? Where are you?" I heard a scraping noise in the far corner where we'd set up the grid, but it wasn't on, so I couldn't tell exactly what the noise came from. I stood still and listened, I heard it again. I turned my head in that direction and saw him then. He was in the far corner, the one that was partially made of earth. I stepped closer to him, but I couldn't see much. He was pressed close into the corner and wasn't moving.

"Jason?" I called again. He slowly raised his hand and started clawing at the wall, the light illuminating enough to show me his fingers were already scraped up from ragged bricks, dirt caked in his nails, and still he hadn't moved. "What are you doing?" I stepped close enough to put my hand on his shoulder. He startled before he froze in place, and slowly turned his head so I could see his face. A slow smile spread across his lips, but it wasn't my Jason who looked back at me.

I jumped back, startled by what was right in front of me. I scrubbed at my eyes, but still nothing had changed. He looked like Jason, but somehow, I knew he wasn't. He turned around and took a step closer to me. "Don't be like that, baby, come here," he purred.

"Get out of him!" I yelled. I wasn't sure what to do. My instinct told me to get the fuck out of here, but my heart wouldn't let me. My mind raced, trying to come up with some way to save Jason from whatever was in control of him, and not hurt him at the same time.

"Wade, the salt, throw some salt at him," a child's voice said to my right. I glanced in that direction but didn't see anything. I backed away from Jason, afraid to turn my back on him, but needing some distance between us. He hadn't moved, he stood in front of me, still wearing that not-quite smile, and breathing so heavily, his breath panted in and out of him as his chest rose and fell in quick succession. I slowly made my way to where we'd put our backpacks down on the crate. Without taking my eyes off him, I felt for the bag of salt. My fingers brushed it, and I lurched toward it to get a better grip before shoving my hand into the bag. Not thinking about it, I flung a handful at Jason. As soon as it hit him, a screeching noise tore through the area and seemed to circle the room, before silence once again fell on the room.

Jason collapsed onto the ground, his hands clutching at his head. "Jason." I rushed over to him and pushed his hands away. He fought me at first, but then he chanced a look, and realizing it was me, he sprung up and pulled me to him. "Are you okay?" I asked, smoothing his hair back and forcing enough distance so I could get a look at him.

He didn't answer at first, he looked terrified, and I had no idea what was really happening.

"Wade, it happened again, it took over my body. I couldn't stop it," he whispered, and glanced around the room.

"Who? I don't understand how this could have happened. We did everything we were supposed to do."

"This is different, Wade, this one doesn't play by the rules. I don't think it knows there are rules. And I know it doesn't care who it hurts, or what it has to do to get what it wants."

"What does it want?" I asked, afraid to know.

"Everything," he whispered, his eyes wide with fright, as his lips quivered. I reached for his hand, and my helmet light went out, once again plunging us into darkness.

CHAPTER TWENTY-SIX

JASON

I BLINKED MY EYES REPEATEDLY, but it was so dark in the basement I couldn't tell the difference between my eyes being open or closed. "Wade," I whispered, "we need to get some lights on." I fumbled with my headlight and pushed the button repeatedly, with no success.

"Stay where you're at, I'm going to see if I can make it to the bags and get a flashlight," Wade said.

"No, don't go alone. We stick together, remember?" I reminded him. We both stood, and after taking a moment to get our bearings, we moved toward the direction we thought the bags were, sliding our feet along the dirt floor and hoping not to trip on any of the boxes stacked around the room.

"It seems like we should be close," I said, feeling around with my foot but not making contact with anything.

"Yeah, this place isn't that big, let me try my headlight," Wade said. I heard him fumble with the button, and this time the light pierced the darkness, startling the two of us. Neither of us moved as we looked around the space, making sure we were indeed still alone.

"Let's finish setting up, we can put a camera in two opposite corners and cover the whole space. Did you bring the EMF detector?" I asked, reaching into my bag and taking out a flashlight. I breathed a sigh of relief when it came on and illuminated even more of the area.

"Yep, got it right here," Wade answered as he took out the device. "Should I turn it on?"

"Yes, maybe we'll have a little warning, it couldn't hurt." I watched as he switched it on. It came to life immediately, detecting a strong electromagnetic field, its lights flashing as it emitted a loud chirping sound.

"Do you think there's electrical wiring or other interference?" Wade asked, waving it around as he turned in a circle.

"I'm not sure, there shouldn't be much electrical down here, the breaker box is in the kitchen. I checked for it when we came before." He continued to watch the meter as I gathered the tools we'd need to anchor the cameras.

"Here's a flashlight. I think we should both place each camera, that way if the flashlights go out, we'll at least be close enough to find each other." He nodded his agreement and we walked over to the corner closest to the door. "If we put it here, it'll be focused on the door and the room," I said.

"Sounds good," Wade said, before helping me find an anchor point and turning the camera on. "Jimbo, how's that look?" I said into the walkie, and waited.

"Yeah, man, looks good. You're putting one at the other end too, right?" he asked.

"Yes, on our way to do that right now." Wade helped carry the tools and camera equipment to the far corner. The closer we got, the thicker the air seemed to get. "Be careful, let's not take any chances," I said, and reached out to tug on

Wade's arm. He slowed and stood closer to me, and we slowly made our way to the back corner.

"Jason, let's get this set up and go back closer to the door," Wade said quietly, and started to attach the anchor for the camera on the wall. I held it steady while he clipped the camera into place and turned it on, then he adjusted the angle.

"Jimbo, how's it look?" I said into the walkie. Nothing. I met Wade's eyes and we waited a second longer. "Jimbo?"

"Let's move back to the door," Wade said, looking uneasy.

"Jimbo?" I tried again, as we made our way out of the corner and into the middle of the room. Finally, when we were in the middle of the room, the walkie crackled to life.

"Jason? Wade? I can't hear you, answer me, you fuckers."

"Whoa, language," I said back to him.

"Jason, you scared me to death. I could hear you clicking in to talk, but nothing was coming through," he explained.

"We have it all set up, can you look at the camera feeds to make sure you can see the whole room now?"

"It looks good from here, I can see it all. Are the lights out?"

"Yes, as soon as we got down here, they went out. We've got our flashlights and headlights so we're good for now."

"Is Wade safe? Don't leave him alone down there, Jason."

"Don't worry, he's right here next to me." I reached out and squeezed Wade's shoulder, needing to remind myself how close he really was.

"Did anything happen when you were putting up the

cameras?" Jimbo asked. Wade's eyes met mine and he shook his head slightly.

"No, nothing unusual. I'm going to sign off for now so we can finish salting this area. Stay close, Jimbo."

"Will do," he said, and the walkie was once again silent.

"I don't want to worry him about what happened earlier, we'll deal with whatever is down here and get the hell out. You and me, Jason, that's all we need to take care of this."

"I hope you're right, I really hope you're right." We moved closer to the basement door and where we'd left the backpacks. I picked up the bag that held the salt and took it out. "We need to salt this area, I feel like we're forgetting something, but I don't know what else we can do."

"Jason, are you sure you're okay? You do understand what happened earlier? You haven't even mentioned it."

"I know what happened. I don't understand why, though. I have the stone Janis said would protect me from being taken over again, I wonder why it didn't work?"

"She said this spirit is different, but how? It's stronger, or maybe it's not a spirit," Wade said.

"She said we needed to do a cleansing, we did it. She said we needed to bring the stones she'd chosen for us, we did. She said we should all be here during the cleansing, we were. What did we miss?" In my mind, I went over what she'd said—*It won't be easy, first you'll need to go to the basement at the restaurant. There you will do a cleansing ceremony. It may not be as easy to cleanse this space as it will be in your own home, and it may take several times. The three of you should be in the spirit circle, along with the owner of the restaurant. You'll need the help of someone who is tied to the building. And for your own sakes, bring your stones, you will need them.*

"Oh god," I breathed out. We'd fucked up.

"What is it? Did you remember something?" Wade asked.

"Yes, and Jimbo isn't going to like it."

CHAPTER TWENTY-SEVEN

WADE

WHEN JASON HAD TURNED to face me from the corner of the room, I knew in an instant it wasn't him. The look he'd given me was pure evil, not the Jason I knew and loved. He hadn't talked about it since it happened, but it had to be scaring the shit out of him. He'd been visibly shaking and sweating since it'd happened, and I knew he felt like he'd done something to contribute to all the trouble we'd had, but he hadn't.

"Wade, we'll need to cleanse this area again, did you bring your stone?" he asked.

"Yes, I wasn't sure if we'd need it, but I was paranoid to not bring it. I've kept it in my pocket since Janis gave it to me."

"Me too. I can't believe I forgot about the spirit circle, we need to do everything again, and we need to do it down here," Jason explained. "Did we bring some smudge sticks?"

"Yes, we packed everything we've used in the past," I answered.

"Good, we're going to need it." He pressed the button on the walkie as he met my eyes. "Jimbo, you there?"

"Yeah, man, just watching you two on the live feed," he answered.

"You're not going to like this, but you and Dean need to come down, I'll explain when you get here."

"Fuck, are you sure we need to do that?" Fear and doubt were evident in his voice.

Jason's gaze never left mine when he answered, "Yes, I'm sure."

A few moments later, we heard them coming down the old wooden stairs, and the door creaked open. There was an intake of breath, probably from the shock of seeing how dark it was down here.

"Stay there, I'll bring you a flashlight." I walked toward them with the bag that held the lights.

"Thanks, man, I left my light upstairs. Not gonna lie, I'm freaking out a little," Jimbo whispered, and stepped a little closer to Dean.

"I know, but it'll be all right, we should have done what Janis said the first time. Jason remembered what we forgot. He'll explain it all." I nodded to where Jason stood to the side with his headlight still on.

"What's going on, Jason? We both know I shouldn't be down here," Jimbo whispered, and looked around the dark space.

"We need to cleanse the area again, and do it exactly like Janis told us to. We forgot to hold a spirit circle, I think that may be what will force the spirits out of this area," Jason explained.

Jimbo glanced at Dean and leaned closer to Jason. "You do realize what will happen if I lose control? This is not safe, Jason."

"I know, we'll do the cleansing, and hurry to do the circle. I'm sorry, Jimbo, but it has to be done." Jimbo nodded but didn't say a word; Dean looked back and forth between the two of them.

"Should I be worried?" he asked.

"We'll know soon enough," I said, and took out the smudge sticks and a lighter. I lit one and handed it to Dean. "Stick together. You two take this area, Jimbo knows what to do. We'll do the back corner." I caught the shocked look Jason gave me before he could hide it. He only hesitated for a moment before he was at my side. We moved quickly through the far area, making sure the smoke filled every nook and cranny within reach, and backing away from the wall and toward the center of the room. We finished the back corner with no issue and met Dean and Jimbo back by the crates.

"What's next?" Dean asked. He looked excited, maybe it wouldn't be so bad having him down here. As long as Jimbo could keep his emotions in check, everything should be fine.

"Now we need to do a spirit circle, a more intense cleansing," Jason explained.

"It will help us focus all of our energies to force the spirit out that's not willing to leave, it won't be able to hide, and it won't be able to resist the pull of our combined power. But we'll have to work together to cloak Jimbo. If the spirit realizes he can draw other spirits here, it may use that to trap even more, and draw more power off of their essence," I said.

Jimbo once again looked worried. Dean noticed the same time I did and squeezed his hand.

"Dean, do you have your stone?" Jason asked.

"Yes, I've carried it every day since you guys gave it to me, I figured it couldn't hurt."

"Good, we'll need it later. First, we need the remains of

both smudge sticks. Jason, are you okay to close the circle?" I asked. He looked a little unsure for a moment, before he picked up the bag of salt.

"Everyone stand together, I'll pour out a circle. Once it's sealed, we cannot cross the line," Jason warned. We all watched as he poured out a thick line of salt in a circle around us. There was a small box in the center, and I took out a small metal bowl and set both smoldering smudge sticks in it. The smoke wafted around us in the closed area, and the salt made it feel like we were somehow enclosed by an invisible wall.

"Take a seat in a circle around the bowl, we'll need to put our stones in it," Jason said, as I took out a few small candles.

"What are those for?" Dean asked.

"They'll help focus the energy, and draw whatever energy is available in the area to us," Jason explained.

We all did as directed and sat cross-legged in the center of the circle, facing the little shrine we'd made.

"Okay, everyone ready?" Jason asked.

"Yep," I said, and took his hand.

"Sure," Dean said, and looked between the two of us.

"Fuck, here we go," Jimbo said, and wasn't the least bit subtle in reaching for Dean's hand.

"We got this," I said to everyone.

"I hope we do," Jimbo mumbled.

CHAPTER TWENTY-EIGHT

JASON

"WE CALL on the spirits that reside in this basement, show yourself," I said, aiming for a serious tone, but sounding like an idiot. I looked at Jimbo, his mouth was hanging open, brows pushed together in annoyance, before shaking his head and looking away. Wade wasn't so subtle.

"What the fuck? What was that?" he asked.

"Just trying to be serious and professional," I explained.

"Well, don't. Okay?" he said, with a shake of his head and a barely concealed grin. "Just do you, stop with the dramatics."

"All righty, then, is anyone there? We want to help you, but we need to talk to you first. Show us how to help you." There was nothing at first, the room was still silent, except for the EMF meter beeping now and then, suddenly it came to life. "What's the reading on that?" I asked Wade.

He didn't answer but pointed his thumb toward the ceiling. It was high, a really high reading. Dean looked between us all, not seeming to know who to look at or what to pay attention to. "Are you here?" I asked.

"Jason, they're here," Wade whispered. I looked around

the room but didn't see anything. I could feel the deep cold that I sometimes felt and didn't realize, until recently, was a sign that a spirit was near.

"Hello, we don't want to hurt you, we just want to help you move on," I explained.

"Jason, they're afraid, something is holding them back. They feel almost desperate to leave, but can't," Wade said.

The room changed, it felt heavier and colder all at once. Jimbo looked even more uneasy. "Jason, something's not right," he whispered without meeting my eyes, as he continued to look around the dark space.

"I feel it too, something's here. It's the same thing I felt when I was stuck in the mineshaft," Wade whispered. His voice quivered; whatever it was, Wade was afraid of it. Really afraid.

"Show yourself, if you're so powerful you can keep all these other spirits in check, show yourself," I yelled, and waited. At first nothing happened. I was about to say something else, when Wade set his hand on my arm.

"Wait, something's happening," he said.

Wade and I were facing the back corner where everything weird had happened so far. I caught a shimmer out of the corner of my eye in that direction. A voice, I could hear it, and looking at Jimbo and Dean, they'd heard it too, only I couldn't tell what it was saying. It was a low whisper, not loud enough to make out, but enough to know it was a voice.

"What the fuck is that?" Dean whispered, turning left and right to look behind him.

"Shhh," Jimbo said, his finger over his lips. "Don't draw any attention to it, they like it. Once they know you can hear them, they always want to communicate." Just as he finished speaking, a blur appeared at the edge of the light cast by the candles. It wasn't big, maybe four feet high, and still had no real form. But somehow, I knew exactly who and what it was.

"Emma?" Wade asked. I turned my head to look at him before turning back to look in the direction his eyes were locked. "Why are you here?" he asked, and never took his eyes off what still looked like a blur. "How can we help?" His expression held so much grief. I wasn't sure why, but seeing him in pain hurt me on a level I had no way of preparing for. I reached my hand out and took his. He didn't look away from the spirit, but he squeezed my hand so tight it nearly hurt. But still I held on, hoping that somehow this was helping, but knowing he was so focused on the spirit, he only knew I was here through my touch.

"What do you mean he doesn't know what he's done? I don't understand what you mean," Wade said, answering some unheard question.

I pulled my gaze away from the blur to find Jimbo white-faced and shaking. Dean put his arm around him and whispered what I thought must be reassuring words, close to Jimbo's ear. His eyes met mine, and I knew, in that moment, that Jimbo wouldn't be able to keep it together. He was struggling with his fear, and his need to stay here and make sure we were all safe, especially Dean.

"Jimbo? Are you okay?" I whispered to him. He squeezed his eyes shut and leaned closer to Dean. He nodded his head but continued to visibly shake and lean into Dean.

"Jimbo, you know what will happen if you don't control it," Wade said.

I turned my head to look at him, and now his complete attention was on Jimbo. "Emma says that's what it wants. For you to lose control so it will have enough energy to get to me. It'll destroy me, Jimbo. You have to hold strong. Can you do that?"

I was so shocked by his words I couldn't react, all I could do was continue to stare, and hope like hell that never happened. "Wade? I don't understand what the fuck is going on!" I yelled, as I fought to stay in control of my emotions.

"You were right, Jason, it wants me. It thinks it can use my body to cross over into the living world again."

"Is that possible?" I asked. I was so shocked, I couldn't think based on any bit of logic. If it, whatever *it* was, thought I'd let it take Wade from me, it was in for a big surprise, because it was about to have the fight of its existence. "What do we do?" I was starting to feel like Jimbo looked, I could feel the color drain from my face, and the cold grip of terror wrapped around me. I started to shake uncontrollably, and my teeth chattered. My gaze flicked between Jimbo, Dean, and Wade, not knowing what I should do, or who to turn to, to make this nightmare end.

The room went silent once again, only this time it was a heavy, dark silence. The room beyond the candlelight was bathed in a dark so inky black, my sight couldn't penetrate it, no matter how hard I tried to focus my vision. The salt barrier started to glow. Dean noticed it and flinched away from it.

"Don't touch it, I'm not sure what's happening," I said. I was supposed to be the one who knew what to expect, but none of this was anything I'd ever seen or read about. I realized Wade had loosened his grip on my hand and turned to look at him.

He sat with a frozen look on his face, staring at a point a few feet above Jimbo's head. His eyes held a now familiar fear. I couldn't tear my eyes away from his, but I knew there was something I was missing, something he knew, and was terrified by the knowledge.

Slowly he raised the hand I did not hold, and I noticed how badly he shook. He pointed to the spot he'd been focused on a moment ago, his mouth opened, but no words came out. I looked to the spot above Jimbo's head, and what I saw made my blood run cold. A face. The shape of a head, neck, and shoulders seemed to press into the spirit circle, somehow using the power we'd gathered for protection to show us its actual form. The shape was too transparent to make out much detail, other than it appeared to be a male entity. It stretched farther into the circle and slowly turned its head and looked at each of us with eyes we were barely able to make out.

All of us were focused on the vision we were seeing, and none of us seemed able to move and react to it. After looking at each of us, a smile appeared on its face, and it pulled away and disappeared. I forced myself to wrench my eyes away from where it had appeared and looked around at the others.

"We need to get the fuck out of here, I'm not kidding, guys. This is dangerous for us all," Jimbo said. No one answered for a moment, all of us still in shock and trying to process what we'd just seen.

"You might be right, but if we don't try to get it to cross over, it never will. And the longer it's here, the stronger it gets. It thinks it just hit the mother lode, catching the three of us here at once," Wade said. I still couldn't wrap my mind around how in tune he was with the spiritual realm. "We can't leave, we have to fight, and we have to win. Because if we don't, there may not be another chance." He looked to all of us.

Jimbo straightened, and seemed to force himself to find

some strength. "Wade, whatever you need, man, I'm here. We'll do whatever it takes to makes sure that asshole stays out of our world and crosses over to where he should be."

Everyone was focused on listening to Jimbo when there was a loud thud directly behind where he was sitting. It was obvious we'd all heard it, but no one seemed to know where the noise had come from. Suddenly Jimbo seemed to be pushed forward, and narrowly missed crashing into the bowl that held the candles and stones. He scrambled to sit and scooted to the side. Behind him, two transparent hands seemed to push through the salt barrier and reach for him. He dove toward Dean and pulled him closer to where Wade and I sat.

"Fuck it, let's do this. This asshole needs to go," Jimbo said, and pulled Dean into his arms.

CHAPTER TWENTY-NINE

WADE

I DIDN'T UNDERSTAND why Emma picked me to reach out to, maybe she knew it would be easier for some reason, or maybe she just chose me for her own reasons. Either way, she had spoken to me. I could see her standing outside our spirit circle, as clearly as if she were alive—long hair in braids, wearing an old-fashioned dress, the same as she'd looked when we'd seen her at The Vineyard House. But why was she here? I tried to ask her, but she wouldn't let me. She spoke quickly and left no room for discussion.

"Wade, I know you don't want to believe what I am about to tell you, but you must. I'm afraid if you do nothing, you will cease to exist, and he will take over your body and your life." I asked her a few questions at first, but soon realized I didn't need to speak, she knew what I was thinking.

"Who is it? Why did he jump into Jason before if he wants me?" I asked.

"I think he wanted to see if he could do it. He's wanted to try for many years, but hadn't found the perfect host," Emma said.

"Who is it, Emma?"

"I can't say, he's forgotten who he was, now he's only hate and fear."

"Can we make him leave? Will he move on?" I asked, hoping it was possible.

"You can, but it will not be easy. He won't want to leave what has taken him so long to build."

"You mean all the souls that he has kept bound here?"

"Yes, he was alone and lost for so long. He did not understand that he should have moved on. He stayed and wandered for many years. He believes we left him, but it's not true. He does not understand."

"Why wouldn't he move on?" I asked, not understanding at all what she meant.

"You will need to trap him, the same way you did at the old house. I was trapped there before you released us. Thank you for that."

"If it released you, why are you here? Shouldn't you be in another realm, or somewhere other than Sacramento?"

"I cannot, my soul is tied to him. I can do nothing until you release him and set us all free." She turned in the direction of the back corner, as though someone had called her name. "I have to go, he'll be angry if he knows I'm here. He can never know I've helped you." She turned once more and walked quickly away from us.

"Wait, Emma, don't go yet."

"Bye, Wade, and be careful," she said as she slowly faded out of view.

"Wade, what the fuck is going on?" Jason yelled as he shook me. It was like waking up from a dream, except I hadn't been asleep. No one else seemed to notice Emma had even been here. And then all hell broke loose! A dark shape shoving its way into the spirit circle, showing us without a doubt how strong it was. Jimbo was visibly shaken, but still tried to keep it together. Dean didn't seem to know what was going on, but when he saw Jimbo's reaction, it seemed to ignite his fear.

"We can't leave. I know you all want to, but I wasn't kidding, it wants us all and it's willing to do whatever it takes to get what it wants. Emma told me what to do, we have everything we need, and it's best we do it before it figures out what we're doing," I explained. I didn't want to give too many details in case somehow it was listening and knew what to expect.

"We all need to calm down and work together. Jason, remember what we did in the basement of The Vineyard House?"

"You mean the—" He left his question hanging as I put my finger to my lips to silence him. I nodded in answer.

"We'll need to do the same thing, only this won't have an exit, it will have one way in." I lowered my voice even more. "We'll only get one chance, then it'll be onto us. We can't mess this up, guys." Jason took my hand and squeezed it. Jimbo still looked terrified but nodded his agreement. Dean looked between us all and slowly nodded along.

"What do we do first?" Jason asked, which was odd since usually he was the expert. Funny how the spirits seemed to decide to give me the information. I knew so little about this stuff, I was dependent on Jason's vast knowledge of all things paranormal.

"We'll need to make an outline of salt and put a candle in the center to draw it there," I said.

"It might be a good idea to put one of the stones in the middle too, it'll be drawn to that power even more than the candle. That may be what drew it to the circle," Jason said.

"Maybe, but mostly it wants us to know how powerful it is so we'll give up and not try to fight it. It's controlled by fear for years, it doesn't seem to remember it was a human at one time. Now its sole purpose is to collect more souls and more power. We need to shake its cage, give it something to worry about."

"You know I'm with you, let's do this. We'll send this asshole back where he came from," Jason said, and stood with his hand out for me. I took it and pulled myself up. Jimbo looked up at us before he and Dean stood too.

"Let's do this, assholes," Jimbo added.

CHAPTER THIRTY

JASON

I PICKED up our stones and passed them back to each of us. Now we knew what to do, and I'd make sure we did it all the right way. I stepped out of the circle and half expected to be attacked, but nothing happened. The room stayed silent, with no obvious paranormal activity.

Wade stepped out next and stood next to me. "I'll get the backpack, it has everything we need."

Jimbo and Dean stepped out and stayed close. The three of us watched as he walked the short distance; we were so on edge, any noise would have set everyone off. But none came, and nothing weird happened. He took the salt out of the bag and handed me the backpack.

"You get the candles and I'll get started on the outline," Wade said as he moved in that direction.

I stopped him with a hand on his arm. "We do this together, remember?" I reminded him, and leaned in to press a kiss to the side of his head. "Together." He smiled in a way that was only for me, and it took everything in me not to pull him into my arms and run like hell out of here. But we were here for a reason, and we'd finish the job. "Dean, you stay here with Jimbo. Actually, why don't you guys stay in the spirit circle, it'll be safer there." I reached out and took Wade's hand and we walked to the back corner. He spread the salt in a half circle, that ended at the two walls of the corner. "Does it need an entrance?" I asked.

"No, it'll come in through the corner," Wade said.

"You're sure?"

"That's what Emma said, I'm just doing what she said to do, hopefully she knows what she's talking about. I really have no clue. You're the expert in the paranormal, I'm just your trusty sidekick," Wade joked.

"You're so much more than that. You always have been, I hope I never made you feel like you were just a sidekick." I still felt so bad about making him think I wasn't interested in him all those years. What a waste of time, we could have been together ages ago if I would have just had the nerve to admit my feelings.

"Baby, you know I'm joking. You never made me feel any way but your good friend. We both screwed up not being honest, but now we have the rest of our lives to make up for it."

"You're right, let's get through this one and start doing some serious living," I said, feeling so much better just knowing we were, as always, on the same page. I took three candles out of the bag and set them in the middle of the circle.

"Remember that symbol you made on the door to the basement at The Vineyard House for protection?" Wade asked.

"Yeah, should I draw one for us here?"

"I think so, maybe on the far wall. Do you know of one that will draw a spirit to it? We could use all the help we can get," Wade explained.

"I know of a summoning symbol, would that do?"

"Sounds perfect," Wade said as he reached in the bag and handed me a stick of chalk. "If you could do it in the middle of the salt ring, that would be perfect."

I cleared my mind and thought about the symbol I needed to draw for a moment. This wasn't the time to make a mistake. This was a more complicated form than the one for protection, with a swirling design that had a Celtic look. I'd never used this one before, and I hoped what I drew didn't end up causing us more trouble than we already had. I finished the design and stood back to check that it was as correct as I could get it.

"How's it look?" Wade asked.

"I think it's good, we can use a candle to increase the power, and maybe one of our stones to draw it in."

"Which stone? I'm not sure which one would be best for that," Wade said. "I know nothing about any of them."

"Use mine," Jimbo said as he walked toward us with his hand outstretched, offering his stone. "It's the strongest between us all, it'll give you the kick you want."

"Are you sure? I know this helps keep you safe, and I'm not sure what's going to happen once we draw it into the circle," I said.

He hesitated for a moment and looked at Dean, who returned his gaze. "I'm sure. Let's kick this spirit's ass back to hell, or wherever it's supposed to be. Just as long as it's not here bothering Dean." He looked to Dean then and gave him a fond smile. I met Wade's eyes and he gave me a similar look.

"Come on, Jason, let's do this," he said. I reached in and lit the candles in the center of the salt circle and set the stone on top of the summoning rune. For a moment it seemed to glow with an energy the room now pulsed with.

"We should get in the spirit circle, we'll be safer there," I said. The four of us made our way back into the circle, the candles still burning brightly, and we all settled back where we'd been sitting before.

"Now what do we do?" Dean asked.

"Now we wait and hope like hell we have enough protections up to keep us safe," Jimbo answered.

We all looked around the dark area, but I wasn't able to see much beyond the two circles, and I doubted anyone else could either. Then something changed; it started with a scratching sound.

"I've heard that before in the restaurant, I thought it was mice," Dean whispered.

"It's not mice," I whispered back, and kept my gaze locked on the other circle. The scratching got louder, more insistent, and seemed closer than it had moments ago. Everyone's attention was on the wall closest to the back corner, where most of the noise seemed to be emanating from. There was a bright flash, and we all cringed away from it. I pulled Wade closer to me, and Jimbo and Dean swiveled to look in the direction it had come from, behind them. I looked over to the corner, and in the center of the salt circle was a glowing orb of light.

"Wade, look," I said, having a hard time staying calm.

"What is that?" Dean asked.

"Come on, let's go check it out." I stood and stepped out of the spirit circle, and the others followed. Wade walked up to the edge of the salt and reached his hand out, as though he was pressing it against a glass barrier visible only to him.

"Jason, we made a mistake. We have to let her go."

"What do you mean? I thought we needed to trap it?" I asked.

"We do, but this isn't the master, or whatever we're calling it today. I know who this is, and we have to let her go. She's scared, and it's slowly draining her power being in there. Soon she'll cease to exist, and it'll be our fault." He sounded frantic to help, but I still wasn't sure why he was so upset. We'd accomplished what we'd set out to do.

"Jason, we have to set her free, it's Emma." Wade reached down and brushed his hand through the salt. As soon as he did that, the glowing orb rushed out of the circle, and Dean was thrown into the wall, hard. He slid down to the floor and didn't move. We stood there in shock for second, and then Jimbo rushed over to his side. Blood was trailing down the side of his face, and he still had not reacted. Jimbo's hands shook as he cradled Dean's face.

"Dean? Can you hear me? I'm here, you're going to be okay," Jimbo said to him as he leaned closer. "Dean?" Still he didn't answer, didn't even move. Jimbo turned to look at us, a frantic look on his face, and his eyes wet with tears. He turned back to Dean, but nothing had changed. "Dean?" He crumpled forward and gently took Dean's hand in his, as I reached for Wade. For just a second we were distracted, and just a second was all it took for the real bad things to start.

CHAPTER THIRTY-ONE

WADE

AT FIRST, I didn't understand what was happening, or maybe I didn't want to believe it. Emma was trapped, and soon she'd be destroyed. Somehow, she'd been drawn into our circle made to trap whatever it was that had threatened us all. I couldn't see her, but I could hear her scream out in pain, and couldn't stand it anymore when she started to fade slowly away. Pulling away the salt was all I could think to do. Thankfully it worked, she'd rushed away and hadn't been completely destroyed. But it had all been a trick. The other entity had used her to enter without us realizing and attacked Dean.

"We need to move him to the circle, something else is here," I said, trying to remain calm, but knowing shit was about to get out of control.

"Wade, can you help me carry him?" Jimbo asked. He looked so devastated, and I totally understood that feeling. He'd brought Dean here even when he didn't think it was safe, because he couldn't tell him no. How many times had I done the same thing just to spend time with Jason?

"Yeah, man, let me help. We really need to hurry, something's here, I'm not sure what, though." Jimbo didn't react, just slipped his arms under Dean's, and I took his legs. We carried him to the spirit circle and set him down on one side. I had stepped inside, when Jimbo set him down and moved just outside the ring. As soon as he was clear of it, a force hit him and threw him back away from the circle.

"Jimbo, are you okay?" Jason asked, and rushed over to him. I was about to follow when I hit the boundary lines of salt and ran into a solid wall. I felt along the smooth surface, looking for a way through, but everything I felt was solid.

"Jason! Jimbo, are you okay?" Jason was still bent over Jimbo, and his breathing had picked up. It reminded me of when Robert Chalmers had entered his body, his shoulders rose and fell with each breath, almost as though he was panting. "Jason?" I tried again.

Jimbo still hadn't moved, but something had shifted in the room; there was an invisible energy I could feel pulsing, almost like a beacon, blinking out a location. Then it hit me: Jimbo couldn't keep his power to draw spirits under control when he was unconscious, and now Jason was trapped out there with him. Exactly what Emma had said would happen was about to.

Jason continued to kneel next to Jimbo but didn't move for a full minute. His breathing continued to be labored and intense. Finally he froze, and slowly turned to look at me. "Wade, can you come here?" he said, wearing a smile that didn't look quite right on his face.

"Jason?"

"Wade, come here," he said again, and this time he turned and started to walk toward me.

"Is Jimbo hurt?"

"Wade, come here. I need you."

"Who the hell are you? Get out of him!" I yelled, unable

to take anymore. It grinned at me, like I'd reacted the way it wanted. It wasn't Jason that was talking to me, I wasn't sure what it was. Something started to move around the basement, a mass of swirling debris filling the room. Jason didn't move, and none of it touched him. Jimbo still hadn't moved, his face turned away from me so I couldn't tell if he was still knocked out.

"Wade, you know what's going to happen, you're going to come out here and I'll take control. I've brought all of my friends to help. They'll make sure everything goes exactly like I've planned," Jason, or the creature who was now Jason, said.

"No, I won't let you take me."

"You know there's nothing you can do to stop it. Now step out of the circle, and we'll begin with me taking over your body—don't worry, you won't feel a thing. Ever. Again." A deep guttural laugh broke through the sound of swirling wind and grew louder and louder. I covered my ears, but it didn't help. "You fool, you're the one I need, this body was just a temporary means to get what I truly want. You're the one with the power, you and that other one there on the floor. With him asleep, I now have more spirits than I'll ever need to exist on this plane forever. No one will be able to stop me. Not ever."

I looked around, frantic for something, or someone, who could help. I noticed Dean's eyes were open, and they were fixated on a point behind me, but I was afraid to take my eyes off Jason for fear whatever was in him would do something to hurt him or Jimbo. Dean met my eyes briefly, before once again focusing his attention behind me. I met Jason's eyes for a second before I glanced to the left. What I saw made me do a double take —dozens and dozens of spirits, all standing crowded around the spirit circle. None of them moved, but they all focused on Dean and me.

"They'll tear that spirit circle apart and you'll be mine," he said with a sneer.

"No, they won't, motherfucker." Jimbo jumped up and punched Jason hard, right in the mouth. Jason's head reeled back from the force of it, and he stumbled backward.

"What? But how? I used your power to draw them all here, you shouldn't be awake," Jason screamed at Jimbo, fury written all over his face. He lunged at him, but Jimbo was faster—which shocked me—and dodged him.

"I'll tell you how, asshole. I know you thought if we'd put our stones in the circle I'd be unprotected, and all you'd have to do was knock me out to use my power," he said as he dodged Jason again and gave him a hard shove away from him. Jason slammed into a crate, and for a moment he seemed stunned. But then he rushed back at Jimbo. "Don't do it, man, I'll kick your fucking ass and you know it."

"Jimbo, don't hurt him, that's still my Jason," I yelled at him, still trying to wrap my mind around what was happening. Dean sat up, rubbed the back of his head and winced.

"Tell him to back off, Wade. He hurt Dean, did you see that shit?" The whole time he was yelling, he kept his eyes locked on Jason, and slowly circled in anticipation of his next attack.

"Jason, stop. What are you doing? Fight it, whatever it is, fight! This isn't you, stop this now," I practically begged. I didn't want to see either of them hurt, but Dean and I were still trapped behind the invisible wall of the spirit circle, so there was nothing we could do besides watch. I pounded on a wall I couldn't see but was as real as if it were made of brick or cement.

"You don't know everything about me, fucker. You think

you can use my ability to draw spirits to you and then use their power for your own. You don't know shit!" Jimbo yelled. I'd never seen him so animated, or so pissed. He shoved Jason back from him again and continued to dodge all of his attempts at restraining him.

Dean's eyes grew wide as he once again looked at the area behind me. I turned to look, and there was Emma. "Wade, I need you to help. We have to make him leave Jason, or all will be lost."

I hit the invisible wall in front of me. "I can't," I said, knowing I was letting us all down, but not knowing how to fix it.

"You can. You know the answer, you can get yourself out of there and save Jason, but you'll need to hurry."

I thought about it for a moment and turned back to Dean. He was sitting up now and looked like he wasn't sure he could trust what he'd just witnessed. "It's real, they can talk to me, and I can hear them," I said to Dean as I leaned down and blew out the candles. The sound that had seemed loud before now increased, and as I moved to cover my ears, I realized the wall was gone. I looked up just as Emma's form seemed to blow away in the wind.

Jason looked at me, and for a moment I knew it was him, and I was willing to fight whoever, or whatever, it took to bring him back to me. "Let's go, asshole," I yelled as I joined Jimbo's side.

CHAPTER THIRTY-TWO

JASON

FOR A WHILE . . . I'm not sure how long, I didn't know what was happening. I was awake, but it was as though I was underwater or waking up from a deep sleep. I knew Wade was there, I could feel him, but I couldn't see him or speak to him. Something happened, and there was pain, white-hot pain. Jimbo—I could see Jimbo—and he was yelling at me. I tried to ask him what the hell had just happened, but my vision was blocked again, and once again I had that sensation of not being conscious in this reality.

"Jason, wake up, asshole. You need to fight. Don't give up, you can beat him," Jimbo yelled, while shaking me. I snapped to attention.

"Jimbo? What's happening?"

"Jason, whatever's down here is trying to use you to get to Wade. If it gets to Wade, we're fucked. You have to push it out of your consciousness. Don't stop fighting, you have to make it clear you're not going to let it take you over."

I closed my eyes and focused. "You won't be able to get rid of me so easily, I've got all the time in the world to get exactly what I want, and there's nothing you can do about it," a strange voice in my head said.

"That's where you're wrong." I reached into my pocket and took out what Janis had said would protect me: black tourmaline. I felt the smooth stone and clenched it in my fist as I removed it from my pocket. Instantly there was a shift, and the pulse of a shockwave hit me.

"Jason? Are you okay?" Wade asked, kneeling next to me and holding my hand. I blinked my eyes to focus, and there he was, just like he always had been. Looking out for me.

"I'm okay, I did what Janis said to do. She was right; the black tourmaline knocked it out of me. Now we need to figure out where it's hiding and make it fucking leave for good." Wade gripped my hand tighter and pulled me to standing. Jimbo was standing close and looked ready to pounce. "It's okay, Jimbo, it's me. Nice right hook, by the way," I said, and stretched my jaw.

"Sorry, man, I needed to keep you focused."

"Yeah, well, good job, I guess."

"Jason, we're not done yet," Wade said as he looked toward the corner where we'd set up the trap.

"It still wants you. It's exactly what Emma said, it wants to take over your body and your life to return to the world of the living. It kept me blocked while it was in me, I couldn't hear its thoughts or what it has planned, but I know it's not good."

"You'll need to draw the spirits that are near and use their combined powers to trap him in the salt circle, that's the only chance you have of defeating him," a female voice said from somewhere near Wade. He looked to his left and nodded.

"Emma said—"

"I heard," I said before Wade could finish.

"Me too, but I don't like it. I'll try to control it, but believe me, we don't want every spirit in this area rushing in here. They'd all overpower us, and we'd never be able to make them leave," Jimbo whispered, and looked over to Dean, who now stood inside the spirit circle. "It's okay, you can come out now. Just stick close."

Dean nodded and stepped next to Jimbo. "Are you okay?" he asked, while brushing his fingers over Jimbo's head. Jimbo ducked his head and nodded.

"I'm fine, I'll be better once all this shit is done. Janis gave me what she said we needed. It's in your backpack, Jason. I didn't want to hide it, but I wasn't sure what your reaction would be. This isn't the type of spirit we've seen before. It's mutated into a force of evil, and we'll need to remove it permanently." He kept his voice down while he talked, and looked around the space, looking for who knew what. "I know that you brought some other forms of protection too, we'll need it all for this to work. And, Wade, we'll need your friend, she may not like it, but she'll have to be bait for the entity."

"Why didn't you tell us all this shit before?" I asked, annoyed that we'd been led into a dangerous situation.

"Because I didn't understand it all until now. You know how cryptic Janis can be. I didn't understand what she meant, but I took the steps she suggested."

"Me too, she gave me a list of a few things she said would be helpful, they're in the bag too," Wade said.

"Am I the only one who didn't have a list of items to bring?" I asked, feeling left out.

"There were things she didn't understand, she told Wade and I what information she could decipher. Maybe she thought it was safer that none of us knew everything,

I'm not sure. Now, we should get ready for what happens next, because it's gonna be a shitshow." I nodded, and Wade took my hand.

"I'll explain more later, but right now we need to get ready. Jimbo, you get the box," Wade said.

"What box? What's going on? When did you two become the experts?" I had to be in an alternate universe, because Wade was no paranormal expert, and Jimbo shied away from it.

"Everyone gather around, I'll explain it all," Wade said. Once we were all in a close circle, he started in a low tone, obviously not wanting anything outside our circle to hear. "We need to trap the spirit in a crystal, for that we'll put the crystal and the box in the trap. It'll need to choose to cross over or to stay. If it won't cross over, we'll seal the crystal in the box and bury it down here where no one will ever find it."

"What is it, Wade? How can one spirit cause so much trouble, and why is it targeting us?" I asked.

"It's a spirit, he died here long ago. He's angry because he thinks everyone he cared about left him to die alone and afraid," Wade said. "He's targeting us because he's drawn to Emma, and she's drawn to us. He was always aware of her, but he didn't know where she was, and when she followed us back from The Vineyard House, he felt her. When she followed along with us, when we came to the restaurant, he felt her, and he trapped her along with the other spirits he keeps here under his control."

"So that's why he wanted Jimbo here, he really thought he could force Jimbo to bring more spirits to him?" I asked, trying to get it all straight.

"He nearly succeeded, some answered his call, but Emma was able to hold them back. To make them pause just long enough for Jimbo to knock the crap out of the spirit, and you." He put his hand to my jaw and leaned in for a gentle kiss. "I'm so sorry you were hurt."

Jimbo rolled his eyes and shifted on his feet. "Can we get this show on the road? I'm ready to be done already."

Dean looked on with a fond smile.

CHAPTER THIRTY-THREE

WADE

I QUIETLY EXPLAINED what would need to happen. I'm still not sure how I knew, but I did, and lucky enough, Jason and Jimbo trusted me. I walked to the backpack and took out the box I'd prepared earlier. It was a plain wooden box I'd filled with a few items guaranteed to weaken a spirit and keep it trapped. I also brought some sealing wax, and a large, clear quartz crystal.

"Jimbo, you know what to do, put the box and the crystal in the trap. Jason, you stay close, and, Jimbo, get ready to use your ability. Dean, you might want to stand behind Jimbo." He moved behind him, and Jimbo reached back and took his hand.

"Everyone ready?" I asked, and everyone nodded. "Emma, are you ready?" I whispered into the dark. There was a brush of wind across my face, and I knew she was there.

"Jimbo, you're on," I said, and watched as Jimbo took the stone he'd retrieved from the circle, out of his pocket, and handed it to Dean.

"Hold on to this for me," he said, with a quick kiss to his

cheek. We all turned to face the darkness that lay beyond the basement walls, and Jimbo bowed his head as though in prayer. When he looked up, his eyes held an intensity I'd never seen in him before, and almost seemed to glow. In one quick motion, he thrust his head back and his chest out, and almost instantly we were surrounded by spirits. They rushed in, crawling through the opening from the outer area, flying around us in a flurry of motion and sound. Mouths agape, and eyes staring at all of us.

"Can you see this?" I whispered to Jason, who looked around the room but didn't seem to see anything.

"No, I don't see anything, but I can feel them. There's a lot of them, a lot," he whispered back.

I kept the same low tone. "They're all around us, hiding us from him. Emma's here, she's by the trap. Be careful, Emma," I said softly. She nodded back to me and turned to face the darkness. For a moment nothing happened, then there was a rumbling under our feet. It was as though a force we couldn't see but could feel was pressing in on us; it would press in, seeming to test its limits, before pulling back slightly. Suddenly it filled the room, and the spirits surrounding us started to scream as they were sucked out of existence. I grabbed Jason's hand and held it tight, hoping we had enough time to trap the entity.

Emma blinked into my vision, right in front of the salt line that defined the trap. All motion stopped, and the mass of power seemed to pause and wait. "Brother, you've waited long enough, come with me and we'll cross over together," she said as she held her arms out in welcome. The rumbling became louder as the mass now took on an inky look, swirling shapes moving through it, and screams filled the area. Then a face was visible, formed in the blackness. The face of a boy. He looked to be a teen, but his features were not defined enough to be sure.

"What do you want, sister? I've waited for you forever, but none of you ever came back for me," he shouted, and the beams holding up the building shook and creaked, dust and debris sprinkled down around us.

"We did not leave you here to die, we left you here when you were sick, too sick to travel. You would have died on the journey to our new home in Coloma."

"But you never returned. I waited, and then the water came." His voice held sadness, but also accusation. "I was washed away, do you know that? My body was carried away in the flood, and ended up in an old mineshaft, where no one would ever find it."

"I'm sorry, Jeremiah, I missed you, we all missed you. And we did look for you. I, too, became ill, not long after you, with cholera, and was buried at our new home. Mother and Father didn't forget you, we were going to come back and get you, when I became sick and was unable to travel. Mother was going to stay with me, and Father would travel back to Sacramento to finally bring you home. But the rains came, and it was so heavy and drenching, Father was unable to pass where the rivers had washed out the roads. He returned home, hoping the weather would clear and he could make the trip at a later date, but I was nearly gone when he returned. He stayed, not wanting Mother to suffer losing another child, alone. When he could finally return, the great flood was upon them, and the Sacramento Valley became an inland sea for many months. They did not want to leave you, it was just beyond their means to get to you."

The black swirling mass stuttered and seemed to lose some of its integrity. But still he did not give up. "None of that matters anymore, soon I'll have enough power you won't be able to stop me." His voice boomed out, as the inky form moved closer to Emma. None of us moved, too afraid he'd see us here among the spirits he was trying to absorb, and worried the plan would fail. Emma looked scared, she raised her arm up as if to protect herself from him, but he remained where he was, not moving closer, and not retreating. Suddenly he seemed to rear back, like a great snake preparing to strike and absorb Emma, but she was too fast for him. Just as he rushed forward to absorb her energy, she disappeared out of sight, and he ended up in the trap.

Through the clear walls it was easy to see him, he swirled around the area, looking for any way out. When he realized there wasn't an exit, he roared out his frustration. The spirits that stood around us all glided forward to look at his form, now safely locked away in the trap of our making. "Emma, are you sure you want to trap him forever? Maybe he'd choose to cross over instead?" I asked, knowing she'd hear me even though I couldn't see her.

"He has chosen, he's too filled with hate and rage to remember the love he once enjoyed. The power he's collected has made him mad, there will be no reasoning with him. This is the only way," she said, sounding sad and defeated. "Use the clear quartz crystal, Wade, you know what to do."

"Jimbo, you ready for this?" I asked. He nodded, and we all stepped over to where the spirits still stood, watching the entity that had threatened to imprison them here for eternity for his own gain. Jimbo once again bowed his head, and held his hand out for Dean, who took it immediately. Suddenly the area was filled with a bright light that seemed to somehow emit from Jimbo. At the same time, the crystal in the trap glowed with the same light, and the light seemed to draw the entity into it. With a loud whoosh, he disappeared. For a moment the crystal swirled with the inky black chaos that had filled the trap only a moment before. The light slowly faded, and all that remained was the crystal and the open box. Jason rushed into the trap and placed the crystal inside the box.

"Can you give me the sealing wax?" he asked, while holding the box closed. I rushed to the backpack and returned with the stick of wax. He heated it over the candle and dripped a large amount of wax on all the edges, sealing Jeremiah's spirit inside. I looked around, and slowly, one by one, the other spirits started to fade, until just the four of us remained.

"Emma?" I said into the dark of the basement.

"I'm here, Wade, I'll always be here. You and I are connected. I will forevermore be your guide to the spirit world. I do this as atonement for the horrible acts my brother has performed while lost in his madness. Thank you, Wade, thank you all. If you need me, you need only say my name."

"Thank you, thank you for everything," I whispered to her.

CHAPTER THIRTY-FOUR

JASON

"WADE, do you think we're safe enough to close the trap now?" I asked, not sure if the process was complete.

"We're safe, let's find something to dig a hole with," he said, and started looking around the basement for something we could use.

"There's a few tools in the space by the door, maybe there's something there you could use," Dean said. I handed the box to Wade, walked over, and found a broom handle that I hoped would help to break up the soil, and a big serving spoon that was stored with pots and pans and other kitchen items. The four of us walked out into the tunnels and chose a place close to the mineshaft. I dug a hole large enough to hold the box, and Wade set it down in the dirt and started to cover it.

"Wait, one more thing, just in case," Jimbo said as he tossed a pink stone on top of the box before it was completely covered. "Rose quartz, it'll repel all negative energy and promote infinite peace and joy." We must have all given him the same shocked look, because he rolled his eyes and explained with a shrug, "Janis's words, not mine."

All of us walked back to the basement area and started to gather up our equipment.

"Wait, is it gone?" Dean asked.

"Yes, there are no other spirits here, they all left when they didn't have Jeremiah tethering them to this spot. While Jimbo has the ability to draw spirits, he cannot force them to stay. Jeremiah was the one holding them all here until he could use their power," Wade explained. "Jason, can you sense any spirits still here?"

I opened myself up to them, tried to be open to feeling them, but there was nothing. They were all gone now. "I don't sense any at all, looks like your place is clean now, Dean. Our job here is done." I smiled at Dean, but a disappointed expression crossed his features. "Is something wrong? Did we do something you didn't want?" I was worried that we'd upset him somehow.

"No, not that. I'm just disappointed you guys won't be around here anymore," he said, and looked around the basement.

"You know I'm still going to be bothering you regularly, don't you?" Jimbo said as he stepped in close to him. "I won't let you get away so easily this time." He leaned in and kissed him with a loud smack, and Wade and I both stood there in shock. Everything about Jimbo was so different when he was around Dean, and all of it was good. He deserved to find his happiness, both of them did.

"Hey, Jimbo, when we get upstairs, let's check your injuries just to be sure nothing more serious happened. We should have done it sooner, but, well, things were a little crazy earlier," I said, jumping back into Boy Scout mode.

"I'm okay, man, let's get this all packed up and get upstairs. I've had enough excitement for one day," Jimbo said, as he and Dean moved toward the basement door and walked up the stairs together.

I started to follow but Wade stopped me. "I need to tell you something . . ."

Worried, I stepped closer to him, and after adjusting my backpack on my shoulder, I pulled him into my arms. "What is it? You're not hurt, are you?" I felt his back with the arm I had around him.

"No, I'm fine, but something happened after Jeremiah was trapped. Emma talked to me."

"What did she say?" My curiosity was piqued.

"She said that we're connected now, and if I ever need help, to call out to her and she'll be there. That she's my spirit guide, and she'll always answer my call." He looked at me, searching for some sign, but not seeming all that sure of himself. I rolled my eyes and pulled him to my chest.

"You always get all the good ghost experiences," I said, and leaned in for a kiss. "I love you, Wade, and I'm so fucking thankful no one was hurt, and you're willing to share my paranormal obsession with me. And it's pretty damn cool that you have a spirit guide of your very own."

"Yeah? I wasn't sure how you'd feel. I know it's always been you that's been attracted to the other side."

"Mostly, I'm just attracted to you, but I do love that we can share our adventures together. Come on, before Jimbo comes looking for us."

He laughed at that, and together we climbed the stairs, back to the world of the living.

EPILOGUE
WADE

IT HAD BEEN two weeks since we'd finished the job at The Hitching Post. Once again, news of our adventures had traveled fast through the businesses of Old Sacramento. Turns out there were a lot of businesses having spirit problems down there. We'd already gone to two other jobs, one at a costume shop that also had a spirit in the basement. It was more mischievous than harmful, and at the request of the business, we left it where it was. The other was at one of the bars, and we'd need to come back and spend more time there to find out what it really was, and what it wanted.

"Hey, want to grab some lunch while we're down here?" Jason asked.

"Sure, let's go check in with Dean." I winked and took Jason's hand. We walked the two short blocks and stepped inside the crowded restaurant. "Is it my imagination, or is it even busier in here now than it was before?" I asked Jason.

"It's really busy, wonder if it has anything to do with their new cook?" Jason said, glancing around the restaurant and at all the full tables.

"Fuck yes, it has to do with their new cook! What's up,

assholes? Come to enjoy my excellent culinary skills?" Jimbo smiled as he clapped both of us on the back. The past two weeks had changed him. Where he was gruff and serious before, now he seemed to smile constantly. He was still an asshole, but he wasn't as grouchy about it.

"Hey, Jimbo, where's Dean?" I asked.

"He's in the office, trying to catch up on his books and staying out from under my feet. Right, Teddy?" Jimbo said to one of the waiters, who hurried by with plates piled high with delicious-smelling food.

"Right, Mr. Jimbo," he said, and hurried off to deliver the food to a nearby table.

"Is it possible to get a table? I guess we would like to 'enjoy your excellent culinary skills'," Jason asked. "I'm starving, so if you could step it up, that'd be great. Not that I'm rushing you or anything."

Jimbo froze and locked his eyes on Jason, not moving for a few seconds, before busting up in laughter I never thought I'd hear from him. "This way, you know we always have a table for you guys."

"So, what are you doing with your place in Coloma?" I asked.

"I found a cook and a manager, I'll try to run it from here, if I can't, I'll sell it. This is where I belong." As he handed us both a menu, Dean walked up, and without missing a beat, kissed Jimbo on the cheek and brushed it with his thumb.

"Thank you, James, you're doing such a great job. Everyone loves the new menu," Dean whispered to him, making him smile once again.

"Oh, you two have it bad," Jason said, and opened his menu to look at all the new items Jimbo had added.

"Yep," Jimbo said, and slapped me on the back before

walking away toward the kitchen with Dean, who turned back to us with a smile and a thumbs-up.

"So, what's next on the agenda?" I asked.

"I'm thinking the brisket dinner sounds good," he said, not even looking up from the menu.

"No, I mean with the business, Running Scared."

"Oh, sorry," he said, closing his menu and setting in on the table. "We'll have to talk to your mom, she's running the show now. I pretty much just leave it all up to her to tell us where to go next. But I do happen to know we've got some exciting stuff coming up." He reached his hand across the table to rest on mine.

"Really, what's got you so excited?" I asked. Funny how, somehow, I went from dreading every job, to looking forward to them. As long as the jobs included Jason, I was more than happy to tag along.

"Someone called with a pretty big job, but we'll need to stay the weekend, and Jimbo will need to go. It's too much for just the two of us. Maybe we could ask Dean too, what do you think?"

"Well, I don't mind, as long as he wants to go, we can start training him on the equipment. Wait, where are we going?" He gave me the smile I loved the most, full of curiosity, adventure, and eagerness.

"Have you heard of Preston Castle in Ione?"

I thought about it for a second, but it wasn't ringing any bells. "Nope, I don't think so. Should I?" I took out my phone, ready to look up some information on it.

"It was a boys' prison, it's closed now, but it's one of the most haunted buildings in the area."

"A prison? Can we handle that?" I asked as I looked at pictures of it on my phone. It was intimidating as hell, and also intriguing.

"Hell yes, we can handle it," Jimbo said, suddenly looking over my shoulder. Then Dean was at his side, squeezing in for a look as well.

"Oh, that looks scary, I'm in," he said.

Jason crossed his arms, leaned back in his chair and raised his eyebrows. "Well, Wade, what about it, are you in?"

I smirked at him before answering. "Hell yes, I'm in. On to the next big adventure."

THE END

ABOUT THE AUTHOR

BL Maxwell grew up in a small town listening to her grandfather spin tales about his childhood. Later she became an avid reader and after a certain vampire series she became obsessed with fanfiction. She soon discovered Slash fanfiction and later discovered the MM genre and was hooked.

Many years later, she decided to take the plunge and write down some of the stories that seem to run through her head late at night when she's trying to sleep.

———————

Contact
Blmaxwell.writer@gmail.com

ALSO BY BL MAXWELL

Also in the Valley Ghosts Series

Ghost Hunted

Jason Thomas had always been obsessed with the ghost stories he'd watched on television from the time he was a kid. He'd always dreamed of visiting those haunted places, and playing amateur ghost hunters with his best friend Wade. As they grew older, Jason's fascination with ghosts grew as well, and he'd drag Wade along to different haunted houses or hotels, always hoping to see an actual ghost.

Wade Rivers loved spending time with Jason, even if it meant he'd have to endure another creepy, supposedly haunted location. Friends since they were kids, and always inseparable, Wade's feelings for Jason deepened from friendship into something more. Unfortunately, so did his fear of the places Jason wanted to explore.

The chance to spend a weekend alone in a famous haunted house was too much for Jason to resist, and almost too much for Wade to endure. He knew going to the deserted house was everything Jason had ever dreamed of, so Wade tried to put his fears aside. But when paranormal things start to happen, admitting to Jason how he feels suddenly isn't the scariest thing Wade will encounter.

Ghost Haunted

Wade Rivers finally has what he's always wanted, his best friend Jason Thomas as his boyfriend. Their first date, hopefully the first of many, starts out with a simple dinner, but Wade has a surprise in store for Jason. They end up at a haunted house exhibit for Halloween.

Wade finds out that Jason loves investigating the paranormal, but he's not as enthused about the other attractions. When they meet up with a fellow paranormal researcher, Jimbo, their fun night gets more frightening with each room in the haunted house.

From the beginning to the end, they'll visit every nightmare imaginable, and they'll all find out some truths about each other they never thought would come to light.

OTHER TITLES

Stone Under Skin

Ankit has lived many lifetimes. Once, long ago, he was made of stone, and marked with symbols and sigils meant to safeguard him and allow him to protect and serve others. He's a living gargoyle now, cursed to live as a human; always watching, at all times aware, and constantly searching for his fated one.

While walking home from his job as a librarian, Ethan Lewis is beaten and robbed. Ankit stumbles upon him, and instantly recognizes him as the man he's fated to. He helps him back to his apartment, and after tending his injuries, watches over him.

Fate has woven their lives together for centuries, but in every lifetime, they could never live freely, or love each other as Ankit has often dreamed of. To change their destiny, they'll fight together with other gargoyles, and a young watcher, who is unaware of the tremendous power she possesses. This will be the last battle against their creator, and they'll either die fighting for their freedom, or survive to live the life they've always yearned for.

Better Together

Since being thrown out of his home by his parents, Caden has been struggling to survive on the streets.

He lives in constant fear, stresses over his next meal, and dreads trying to find a safe place to sleep at night. He eventually finds an unlocked car and settles in to sleep, but is soon interrupted when someone steals the car. With little choice but to ride along, Caden soon learns that first impressions aren't always correct.

Seventeen-year-old Damario has been raising his little brother and sister by himself since his parents were deported. He never knew how hard it was going to be paying the bills and making sure there was always food on the table. Or how hard it would be to hold his family together when they all depended on him to do it. He finds himself stealing cars to make ends meet, but he never expected to find someone sleeping in the back of one of them. And he really didn't expect this stowaway to change his life.

When Damario brings Caden home, it was supposed to be just for a shower and a hot meal, but he can hardly kick him out onto the streets again. There is no way he could have seen that by saving Caden that night, he was also saving himself. When Damario's world starts to fall apart, they both realize that the answer to all of their problems is helping each other, and although the world tries to drive them apart, they really are better together.

Ride

Kace Hallard leaves Sacramento, bound for the Sturgis Motorcycle Rally, something he and his father had always planned to do together. When his father realizes he won't be able to make the trip, he makes Kace promise to go on his own.

He takes off, not sure he's up to the challenge. When he has mechanical trouble a few hours away from home, he questions his choice even more.

Striker Johnson is just out buying lunch for the guys at the shop when he notices the handsome stranger in the parking lot checking over his Harley and looking confused. He approaches him and offers his help.

The next few hours fly by, and Kace asks Striker to join him.

It's the trip of a lifetime for them both, one man looking to ease his grief, the other riding toward emotions he has no hope of controlling. One way or another they'll have to decide if they ride together or separately, when life throws them one more curve.

Salt and Lime

Sal Hutton books a trip to Cancún on a whim. Needing some time off from work, he sees an opportunity to go and takes it— alone. After a red-eye flight and full of excitement for what he might experience over the next week, he strikes up a conversation with the handsome taxi driver who gives him a ride to his hotel, and hopes their paths cross again.

Derrik Green came to Cancún for a vacation, and two years later is still here, after falling in love with the city and its people. He's working as a taxi driver and is happier than ever. After dropping off the man named Sal, he can't stop thinking about him, and hopes that eventually he'll call, even if it's just to hire him for a ride or private tour.

Soon their wish comes true and they're spending time together, enjoying all the sights and adventures Cancun has to offer.

Sal and Derrik weren't looking for love, but maybe they were meant to meet here, half a world away from their regular lives, and right in the middle of a tropical paradise. With so many people behind them, they might just get their happily ever after under starry nights and surrounded by the beautiful blue Caribbean.

Cake Clash

Finn Leighton loves owning his bakery and tries not to dwell on the boyfriend that was the love of his life in culinary school. When his co-worker sends in an application for him to compete on the reality baking show, Cake Clash, he's nervous but also excited for the opportunity. Even if he secretly wishes he was competing alongside Josiah.

Chef Jos, one of the youngest, renowned celebrity chefs, and a notorious recluse, is surprised when he's asked to be a judge on the reality television baking show, but takes the opportunity as a fresh start. He's blown away when he recognizes Finn as one of the contestants.

The years separated from Finn have transformed him from Josiah Stevens to Chef Jos, and seem to disappear in the presence of his first love. Can they make up for lost time, and reconnect for love on the rollercoaster ride that is Cake Clash?

Check Yes or No

Sam and Reese exchanged valentines when they were children, neither realizing how much those simple cards would impact their lives. When fate brings both together again as adults, what started as a friendship grows into more. They celebrate every year on the day that brought them together, Valentine's Day by reading from their first Valentine's and looking back on all the events that have shaped their lives as a couple. Valentine's Day brings them more love and happiness than they could ever have imagined all those years ago

Made in the USA
Las Vegas, NV
06 November 2021

33846775R00111